The Sex Files

K. SEAN HARRIS

Cover concept: K. Sean Harris
Cover Design: Sanya Dockery
Typeset & Book layout: Sanya Dockery

Published by: Book Fetish
www.bookfetishjamaica.com
info@bookfetishjamaica.com

Printed in the U.S.A   ISBN: 978-976-610-799-4

Man's Hierarchy of Needs:
Sex
Food
Clothing
Shelter

Contents

Decisions

I was in the lobby of Kingston's most popular business hotel sipping on a steaming cup of coffee – I consume at least four cups a day – when he walked in. Or strutted rather. He was tall – about six feet, and very easy on the eyes. His penetrating gaze made me uncomfortable. Why the hell was he looking at me like that? I squirmed uneasily on the small chair, wondering why my heartbeat was accelerating. I managed to tear my eyes away and look down into the cup like I had suddenly discovered something very interesting in my coffee. He came over and sat down opposite me. Uninvited. I looked up with what I hoped was a cool, quizzical look.

"Hi, I'm Curtis," he said, extending a large, manicured hand.

"I'm Kayla," I responded, as I shook his hand.

He held it and brought it to his lips, giving it the softest of kisses.

I blushed furiously. Mind you, compared to me, Wesley Snipes looked light-skinned but I swear I flushed pink. I looked around the lobby to see if anyone was watching us. The rotund guy in the ugly pink shirt that had hit on me ten minutes ago was smirking with his friend a few chairs away. I quickly withdrew my hand. Curtis smiled. *Damn he had a pretty smile.*

"I came by the hotel to see one of my friends. He works in the accounts department," Curtis informed me, leaning back in his chair. "But as you can see, I just had to take a detour. I haven't seen a woman as arresting as you in some time. Couldn't take my eyes off you..."

Negro please! Spare me. It sounded pleasing to the ear though. I can't ever recall being described as *arresting.* Cute, sexy, thick, voluptuous, yes; but arresting? That was a new one.

"Is that right," I drawled, struggling to play it cool. I wanted to kiss his juicy lips so bad it was ridiculous. They just looked so scrumptious. And the way he licked them. *Damn!* I needed to calm down before I made an ass of myself. I'm thirty-three years old. Got no business having erotic thoughts about a man I just met. Especially one that seemed to be at least five years my junior. After breaking up with my fiancé, I had found my comfort zone in the church and my sex drive had been practically non-existent for the past two years, despite the subtle and sometimes not so subtle advances from some of my church brothers. Work. Church. Home. That has been the story of my life for the past twenty four months, much to the chagrin of my long time best friend, Tiffany. She missed having fun with her partner in crime.

"I would love to take you out sometime," Curtis said, breaking into my thoughts.

"Curtis," I began, weighing my words carefully. "You seem like a really nice guy but I'm not really dating right now...not interested in a relationship at the moment."

"Ok," he replied, smiling at me like I just told him the best news he'd heard all week.

"No problem...we'll just be friends," he continued. "I'm a firm believer that people enter each other's lives for a reason...all I ask is that we give ourselves a chance to find out what our reason is."

He held out his hand for a handshake.

"Deal?"

I had to laugh. I returned his smile and shook his hand.

"Good...now that that's settled, I'm going to go see my friend for a few minutes. Meet you back right here?" He stood and looked at me expectantly.

"Maybe you'll come back and see me and maybe you won't," I replied, half-teasingly. Part of me really wanted to haul ass and hope I never saw him again. But the part of me that had been dormant for so long had inexplicably been awakened and was pouting that I had better sit my ass down until he returned.

"You'll be here," he stated confidently, his disarming smile minimizing the cockiness of his statement. With that he sauntered off to the administrative block of the hotel.

I sighed and sipped my now lukewarm coffee as I watched his retreating back. The last time a man had such an effect on me was exactly thirteen years ago. When I was twenty, I met this guy named Ray at a shopping mall. I was just coming out of my shell at the time and the guy just floored me. He was just irresistible. Good looking, cocky yet charming, street smart, sexy...I just *wanted* him. I had sex with him two days after meeting him, which is still a record for me up to this day. I had never had sex with anyone without dating them for at least two months. The sex had been off the chain. Ray was a pipe-laying maniac. That man knew his way around the bedroom. We were in a steady relationship for three years and even after he left me for an older woman whose father had died and left her a great deal of money, I still slept with him. It wasn't until he migrated and I was unable to get in touch with him that I was able to break the hold he had on my heart... and my pussy.

***

"What's up man?" Curtis said as he greeted Gregory, his best friend since his third year at university. At first they had been fierce competitors as they were both known for promoting the best parties on campus, but after a year of trying to top each other, a mutual friend suggested they joined forces which they grudgingly did. It had been and continued to be a fruitful partnership. Golden Touch Promotions was one of the most successful promoters on the entertainment scene. They were the pioneers of the 'ultra-inclusive' party concept where patrons paid one cover fee to drink and eat to their heart's content all night. They kept four parties yearly, and they were all calendar events on the local party scene, bringing in a substantial income to the two enterprising young men who also both held good day jobs.

"Nothing much, here dealing with this balance sheet," Gregory replied. "The guy from Miami call you back yet?"

Their second party for the year, and the one which was recognized as the one that kick-starts the summer, was seven weeks away. It had a pirate theme and Curtis was trying to source costumes for the team of twelve women and six men that would be working at the venue.

"Yeah, he is going to fax a pro forma invoice tomorrow," Curtis replied. He glanced at the picture of Gregory's sister, Janelle, on Gregory's desk. He hated having to sneak around with her but they didn't want her doting, older brother to know that she was seeing his best friend and business partner. Gregory was fiercely protective of his sister, especially after their father passed away to prostate cancer ten years ago when he was eighteen and she was thirteen. They had been dating for a month now, two months after he had picked her up from the airport when Gregory had been ill with a nasty bout of the flu. She was returning home from Canada where she had completed her first degree in Interior Design.

"Ok, good. Everything is on stream then," Gregory said clasping his hands behind his shiny bald head as he reclined in the leather swivel chair. "The caterer has sent me the proposed menu and I've already gone through it and ticked off what I agree with...take it home and have a look. It's the final thing left to approve."

Curtis picked up the stack of papers to the left of the desk.

"Alright, talk to you later...I have this hot chick outside in the lobby waiting on me."

They gave each other a pound and Curtis left to go back out to the lobby. He stopped short when the table where the woman had been sitting came into view. It was now occupied by two rather plump ladies who were talking animatedly and digging into assorted pastries. She was nowhere to be seen.

***

I exited the bathroom just in time to see Curtis heading towards the exit. He looked disappointed. I chuckled and walked slowly behind him. I had intended to wait for him at the table but had badly needed to pee. Maybe it was fate why I came back out when I did. A few seconds later and I wouldn't have seen him. And that would've been that.

***

Unaware that Kayla was behind him, Curtis walked briskly to the parking lot. He checked the time. It was almost 4:30 p.m. He wouldn't get back to the office until about 5, depending on the traffic. He was an assistant manager at Spartan Security, the leading private security firm in Jamaica. The upsurge in crime on the island had led to a huge jump in the demand for the company's home security gadgets. He reached his 2006 Toyota Tundra and started it with the remote.

***

"Nice truck," I purred behind him.

He turned around, surprised. He had been so deep in thought that he hadn't realized someone was behind him.

He grinned. "Be careful sneaking up on me like that young lady...I'm strapped."

"Hope you're not firing blanks..." I teased, wondering if he really owned a firearm. Guns excited me. I used to look forward to going to the shooting range on a Sunday with my uncle, Basil, an ex- soldier.

Curtis leaned his fine ass against the truck and smiled at me.

"You were supposed to be waiting at the table...not sneaking up on me in the parking lot..."

"Hmmm...guess I'm not very good at following instructions," I replied, smiling cheekily.

"You deserve a spanking," Curtis drawled, looking directly in my eyes.

I was turned on immensely by the image of his large hands slapping my ample ass. When I had been sexually active, I used to love getting spanked while being penetrated deeply from behind. I wanted to let Curtis grip me with his strong hands and fuck the stuffing out of me. Oh Lord. This was all too much for me. I didn't even know this man.

"You're not getting any Curtis," I said to him suddenly, sounding unconvincing to my own ears.

Curtis moved towards me in response. I backed up a bit.

"What are you doing?" I asked as I backed up against another car. I was trapped. I glanced around the parking lot. There were a few people around but no one was paying us any attention.

"We have this insane chemistry...it's useless to fight it...and why would you want to...you only live once..." Curtis said softly. We were standing inches apart. He brushed my cheek lightly with the back of his hand. I swear to God I shivered.

"I have to go Curtis," I told him, my eyes looking straight ahead at his chest; I didn't trust myself to maintain eye contact.

He then gently kissed my forehead. *Sweet Jesus!* I thought, *not the forehead kiss!* I've always found it to be a very endearing, intimate gesture.

He slipped his business card in the small pocket on my close-fitting blouse. His hand grazed my breasts. My nipples were rock hard.

"Call me...anytime."

With that he abruptly left and hopped in his truck. He blew the horn once and left me standing there horny and dazed. I was still trying to wrap my head around the past forty-five minutes.

How the hell did I go from relaxing and enjoying a cup of coffee and planning to attend Bible classes later in the evening to wanting to have a complete stranger ravage my body? If I had read it in a book I would've been like *yeah right*. But as they say, truth is stranger than fiction. I sighed and made my way to my spacious dark blue Toyota Mark 11. I loved big cars. I loved big dicks even more. I wonder if Curtis...oh Lord. I need prayer.

***

"I missed you today baby," Janelle whispered, as Curtis placed her on the kitchen counter and pulled her panties to the left, freeing her gaping flesh.

"How much?" Curtis growled as he freed his erection and rubbed it up and down against her engorged clit.

"Oh god...a lot ...put it in baby...I want it so bad..." Janelle begged. Her period was due in a couple of days and she was always at her horniest and most wanton at that time. "Fuck me Curtis...like only you can..."

Curtis obliged and slid his lengthy dick inside her slowly. Janelle moaned and wrapped her legs around him, pulling him in as deeply as possible.

"Oohhh...that's it baby...I love it...yes baby...fuck me..." she said as Curtis increased his tempo with each stroke. College abroad had been a liberating experience for Janelle. Away from the over-protective eyes of her older brother, she was free to find herself. And one of the things she discovered was that she loved sex. Often and hard. Fine, available men had not been in shortage on campus and she had indulged. Even dabbled outside of her race on a couple occasions. Boris, a Russian who majored in engineering had been a memorable experience. Unruly blond hair, vivid blue eyes, thick circumcised dick and a tongue that loved to probe *every* orifice. He had truly broadened her horizons.

Curtis pulled out and Janelle slid off the counter and turned around. Curtis squatted and spread her cheeks widely. He then licked and nibbled her vulva from behind. Janelle moaned loudly and her knees buckled as Curtis' tongue and lips worked their incredible magic between her legs.

"Don't stop baby...that feels so fucking good...mmmm... mmmm...I'm about to come baby...that's it Curtis...oh god... I'm coming baby!"

It was a powerful orgasm. One that shook her to the core. She swore her toes curled in the close confines of her black four-inch stilettos.

Curtis rose quickly and rammed his dick inside her pulsating wetness. There was a loud fart-like sound as the air that had gotten inside her exited with Curtis' deep strokes.

"Fucking hell...I'm coming again Curtis...harder...faster!" Janelle screamed as she held on to the kitchen counter for dear life.

Curtis' movements were a blur as his own impending orgasm rushed to the fore. He wanted to pull out but couldn't. He grunted loudly as he ejaculated inside Janelle, clutching her tightly as they both shuddered, reeling from the intensity of it all. What was supposed to have been a quickie – Janelle had a meeting with a young women's professional group in a few minutes – had turned out to be a mind blowing come fest. There was no way she could make it now. She needed to relax for a little while and a shower was also in order. Her shapely thighs were sticky with both their juices.

<hr />

I didn't make it to Bible class that evening. I went home, took a very cold shower, and read a section of the supplement that was handed out a few days ago at church. I then curled up in front of the TV and turned to a movie on Lifetime but I couldn't concentrate. Curtis kept penetrating my thoughts. His card was on the night-table next to my over-sized bed. I have no idea what a five-foot-two single woman was doing with a queen-size bed, but as I said, I have a predilection for big things. I had two choices. I could rip the card to shreds and get rid of my only means of contacting him and get over this insane carnal phase that meeting him had me going through and move on with my life, or I could give him a call and see where this journey would take me.

Decisions. It was amazing how they shaped your life. I remember one evening I was invited to a cocktail reception by Tiffany. Her boyfriend at the time had invited her and told her to bring a friend. The reception was for a non-profit US organization that had a huge budget for a four year project for homeless children in Jamaica. I had been reluctant to attend but Tiffany had begged, saying that her boyfriend would be busy as he was part of the committee that had planned the reception. Going there had changed my life. At the time, I had been employed to a leading commercial bank where I was slowly but surely losing my mind. My supervisor was hell on two legs. There was just no pleasing that woman. She made life very difficult for me on a daily basis. Up to this day I have no idea why she disliked me so much. My co-workers were another story. The men all tried to get into my thongs and the women resented the fact that the men showed me so much attention. The things they said behind my back. Some of the guys, trying to score brownie points would come back and tell me some of the things they overheard: "She ah lesbian" and "She love gwaan like she ah Christian an' look how she love dress up hot and look how her batty big". As if I could do anything about the size of my ass even if I wanted to. Rumors circulated and if you let them tell it, I was fucking a new guy in the department every other week.

I met the project manager, a petite brunette with a ready smile from Indianapolis, at the reception. She took an instant liking to me and told me to send her my resume the following day. They needed to hire six Jamaicans for the project and only two of the posts had already been filled. The project sounded exciting. I loved being around children, I would be making an important contribution to society, I would be traveling all around the island, and last but not least, the pay was very good. I would be earning a little over twice what I was getting paid at the bank.

I had sent her the resume first thing the next morning and in two days I was in an interview with her and the regional manager. The interview went well and I was offered the job. Turning in my resignation to my supervisor had been a very satisfying experience. When she queried where I was going and if I needed a recommendation, I sweetly told her to mind her own business with a bright smile. I have been in the new job for a year and a half now and it has been very rewarding thus far. My spending power is greater than it has ever been, I am energetic and look forward to going to work in the mornings, and I feel much happier in general.

Another good decision was breaking it off with Ralston, the man I thought I would've spent the rest of my life with. To be honest, I didn't love him. But I was comfortable around him, he offered security and I was thinking about the future. Settling down, getting married, having kids, you know, most women's dream – even an independent one such as myself. He cheated on me twice – well I caught him twice I should probably say – and after forgiving him the first time; the second time had been too embarrassing and painful to overlook. The entire apartment complex where he lived, it seemed, had come out to witness my pain. He still calls every now and then but I have learnt not to look back. It will cause you to stumble while moving forward. Ralston, his law degree and his nine and a half inch dick could go to hell. I missed his dick more than I missed him. That shit used to fill me up just right.

I sighed and went into the bedroom to call Curtis. I had a history of making good decisions. Let's hope this one doesn't mess up my track record.

***

After leaving Janelle's apartment, Curtis went home to shower and to relax for a bit. It was a Thursday evening. That meant he and Gregory would be linking up later that night at Bembe, a popular party held every Thursday night on Constant Spring road. It went on from 10 p.m. to 2 a.m. but despite the early ending, the venue didn't get packed until at least 1 a.m. Jamaicans just didn't like to party early. He had arranged for a crew of ten attractive girls to wear T-shirts and hats advertising his upcoming party, and to hand out flyers and other things during the course of the night. He had put Shonda, a cute freshman he had met at the bank the other day, in charge of the crew. Curtis relaxed on his patio and looked through the menu that Gregory had given to him. He agreed with most of the choices that Gregory had ticked off except for two of the chicken dishes that he thought were overkill. His Samsung Blackjack rang as he placed the menu on the small table and lit up a cigarette. It was a private number.

<hr />

I felt nervous excitement as I waited for Curtis to pick up. I was curious to see if I was as affected by him over the phone as I was by his physical presence.

"Hello."

"Hi Curtis. It's Kayla."

"Hi there...I've been waiting for your call," Curtis said, sounding as if he was smiling.

"Sure you were," I remarked sarcastically, noting that my nipples were hardening. Yep, he still had that effect on me.

"Are you calling me a liar, Kayla?"

"I am...and what are you going to do about it?" I challenged.

"Write it down...and punish you appropriately when the time comes..."

My mouth watered as he let the words hang in the air. I wondered what kind of punishment would be meted out to me. I tried to think of a comeback but the sudden surge of moisture between my legs was distracting me.

"Have you eaten yet?" Curtis asked.

"No," I answered reluctantly. I was a bit hungry but was in no state to be going on a date with Curtis at the moment. I was unbelievably horny. It would be easier for George Bush to be

11

re-elected than for me to say no to Curtis if the opportunity arose for us to have sex.

"Good, neither have I. We are going to Gilbert's Wrath. I'll pick you up in an hour," Curtis announced.

Not so fast buddy. "I'll *meet* you there in an hour," I countered.

Curtis chuckled. "Ok, see you in a little while."

We got off the phone and I went into the closet to select an outfit. I chose a red halter top and a pair of khaki capris. I don't know why I chose those capris to wear. Or maybe I did know. It really showed up my assets. My ass and the imprint of my very plump vagina would be on display. The delicious seafood at Gilbert's Wrath - named after the infamous hurricane that devastated Jamaica back in 1988 - wouldn't be the only thing causing Curtis to salivate. I smiled as I looked for my red thong. I must admit, it felt good to be dating again.

Janelle's cell phone rang, startling her. She was lying on her bed. Naked. After Curtis had left her apartment, she had taken a shower and had fallen asleep. She yawned and answered the phone. It was Tiffany. They had met at a party through a mutual friend a month ago and had since become regular hang out partners.

"Hey girl, what's up?" Janelle said, checking the time on the naughty wall clock Curtis had bought for her a couple weeks ago. It had a naked couple in the centre and everytime it reached the hour mark, it would chime and the man would penetrate the woman. It was 8:15 p.m.

"I need a drink...I had a shitty day at work," Tiffany told her. "Super bitch was there today."

Janelle chuckled. 'Super bitch' was the marketing manager for the cellular network where Tiffany worked as assistant store manager at their New Kingston branch. She always managed to get under Tiffany's skin whenever she visited the branch.

"I need to be like you girl and start doing my own thing," Tiffany said wistfully, though they had become close enough to know that Tiffany would not leave the security of a monthly pay-check to start her own business. Since returning to Jamaica with her degree in Interior Design, Janelle, with her brother's help, had started her own business and after a slow start, things were picking up quite nicely as the word spread about her reasonable prices and natural flair for design.

They both laughed. Tiffany really liked Janelle. Though Janelle was six years younger, she was very mature and balanced for her age. She was extremely focused yet still found time to have fun, and lots of it. Best hang out partner she'd had since Kayla got all religious on her.

They chatted for a few more minutes before Janelle told her she was going back to sleep. Tiffany teased her that her mystery man was wearing her little ass out and Janelle laughed and hung up. Janelle hadn't told any of her friends who she was dating. Curtis was a very popular guy around town and she didn't want to risk her brother hearing about it yet. She would tell him after they had been seeing each other awhile longer. She was now a grown woman and could see whomever she wanted but she respected her brother and knew that he wouldn't approve of her dating his best friend. They were two of Kingston's most popular young men in a lot of circles, and it was widely said that Curtis was the wilder of the two. Gregory would hit the roof. Janelle sighed and pulled the covers. It was only 8:30 p.m. but she was very tired. Four orgasms after a hectic day at work could do that to a woman.

Curtis and I arrived at Gilbert's Wrath a few seconds apart. I was standing at the door scanning the place when I felt his hand casually drape my shoulder.

"Looking for me?" he breathed in my ear. He smelled so good. I tried to guess the scent he was wearing. It might have been Desire by Dunhill, but I wasn't sure.

"Maybe..." I replied, looking at him. He apparently looked good in anything he wore. He looked absolutely delicious in his fitted Lacoste polo-type shirt, slacks and Gucci loafers.

He smiled and lightly held on to my fingers as he led me to a corner table. Gilbert's Wrath was a very expensive but laid back seafood restaurant that had the best grilled lobster in town. Their salmon salad was also to die for. As usual, there was a good amount of people there dining. The owner, a short, stocky, friendly half-Chinese man who had lost his two businesses when Hurricane Gilbert had struck the island 19 years ago, must have found it sweet irony naming his new successful business after the hurricane.

We sat and a waiter immediately came to us. He knew Curtis. They exchanged pleasantries and Curtis ordered their famous grilled lobster for both of us. The waiter brought us fish tea and soft rolls while we waited.

"Let me do that for you," Curtis suggested.

I cocked my waxed eyebrows quizzically. "What?"

He leaned over in reply and sensuously used his tongue to lick my lips. I was too shocked and embarrassed to react. I was sure people saw us. I dared not look around.

"Curtis!" I said in a loud hiss.

He smiled as he looked at my chest. "*They* approved," he murmured.

I didn't have to look down to know that my nipples were erect and straining against my halter top. I could feel them.

"You crazy, crazy man," I said as I looked at him.

"If all your lips taste that good I just might get hooked," he teased, as he leaned back in his chair.

"If you lick all my lips as well you just did, *I* just might get hooked," I replied saucily.

Curtis found that hysterically funny for some reason. He laughed so hard I had to join in. By then our food was ready and we dug in enthusiastically. Turned out we were both seafood lovers of the highest order. By the time dinner was over, and we were talking over drinks, I was sold. Charming, witty, good-looking, tall, well-built, plus the full blown chemistry between us...I was ready for him to end my two year drought. He said he had a bonafide girlfriend but that she lived in the States. When I asked him how many women he was currently sleeping with, he answered by saying admittedly, pussy was the least of his problems but that he didn't sleep around indiscriminately. All of that didn't matter right now. I had decided to give it up. I could live with whatever happened after. I was a grown woman making a conscious decision.

We walked out to the parking lot, lightly brushing against each other. Nothing was said but it was obvious that Curtis considered it a done deal, when he turned to me and casually asked "Your place or mine?"

I wished I had the willpower to make his too-confident ass wait a little longer but I was never one to cut off my nose to spite my face. I wanted him as much he wanted me. My pussy was hot, wet and ready to be filled.

So I smiled and told him his place. He would get to know my apartment in due time, depending on the how the next few hours unfolded. He gave me his address and hopped into his truck. He headed out into the light Thursday night traffic on Holborn Road and I eased out behind him, bobbing my head to Green Day's new single. I love alternative music. Curtis had a heavy foot. I lost sight of his truck when I got on to Waterloo Road. No worries though, I knew where to find his apartment complex easy enough.

It was a swanky, new, mid-size complex located in Constant Spring. The security guard at the entrance apparently was expecting me and waved me through with a smile. Each apartment was allotted two parking spots so I slid into the vacant slot next to Curtis' truck at apartment D. He opened the door as I stepped onto the patio. He was wearing a white terrycloth robe and Prada house-slippers. I had to smile. Curtis was something else.

He grinned and moved aside, gesturing for me to come in.

I entered and he closed the door behind me. My eyes wandered around the living-dining room. It was contemporary and stylish. African masks and expensive-looking paintings adorned the walls; there was a slick wine cabinet in the right hand corner next to a red leather futon, a large entertainment centre with a 36" inch flat screen TV and a sleek-looking stereo was the focal point of the room.

He took my hand and led me to the bedroom. My heart raced. *Not wasting any time are we*, I mused inwardly as we went into his fabulous bedroom. There was a white silk robe on the king-size bed.

He hugged me from behind and gently nuzzled my neck. I could feel his manhood on the small of my back.

"Put that on and come join me in the bathroom," he whispered, as he gave my right ass cheek a light slap and sauntered off into the bathroom.

I undressed slowly. I haven't had sex in two years. I intended for this experience to be a memorable one. That meant a slow, tantalizing build-up was in order. I admired my naked form in the large wall to wall mirror on the right side of the room. Even in the soft light I could see that my clit was already erect. I touched myself. I was ridiculously wet. I slipped on the robe, and went into the bathroom to join Curtis.

He was chilling in a Jacuzzi sipping champagne from a glass. The bathroom was large, and the area where the Jacuzzi was located was sectioned off from the toilet and shower area by a titillating erotic-themed stained glass door. Scented candles bathed the room in a soft glow. He stood and held out his hand for me to join him. I chuckled when I looked at his groin. He was wearing a cock ring. I had seen pictures of them online but I had never actually seen one on a man's dick before. Curtis was a freak. Good. So was I.

I slipped off my robe and stepped into the Jacuzzi. Instead of taking his hand, I reached for his dick. It was so fucking hard. Though his body was wet from being in the Jacuzzi, I lubricated my hand by swiping my pussy and started to stroke him. He liked that.

His dick swelled in my hand. I cupped his scrotum as I stroked him. He reached for the bottle of champagne and poured some on his dick. I immediately squatted and started to lick his genitals.

He moaned loudly.

"Your mouth feels so good...mmmm...damn..."

I licked and nibbled along the impressive length of his shaft before demonstrating my deep throat skills. I swallowed all of it. Curtis' knees buckled from the shock and pleasure of seeing his long dick buried to the hilt in my mouth. I held it for several seconds before coming up for air. It brought out the animal in him. He growled and pulled me to my feet. He kissed me roughly and then made me sit on the edge of the Jacuzzi with my legs spread. He knelt in front of me and proceeded to eat my pussy like it was his favourite dish. He was excellent. He varied his technique until my body told him what it liked. A man with a hurricane tongue who pays attention. That's a good combo. When the first orgasm hit me, I wailed like a banshee. I had not had an orgasm in two years and this one was as intense as any I could remember. I couldn't stop screaming or trembling. Curtis' magic tongue didn't let up. He kept going like the energizer bunny and I had to beg him to stop after the fourth orgasm made me feel faint. It was unbelievable. My pussy felt like it didn't belong to me. When he finally stopped, I slid into the water and sat with my back against the wall. The hot water felt good on my sensitive clit and throbbing pussy. I sighed contentedly and indicated for him to give me some champagne. He started to reach for a glass but I gestured impatiently for him to give me the bottle.

I took a long swig. Curtis grinned and reached for a condom. I stopped him in his tracks.

"Did I tell you I was through sucking you?" I asked saucily. Curtis smiled. He then stood directly in front of me and placed his right leg on the edge of the Jacuzzi. I put the bottle down and attacked his turgid dick. I sucked him noisily as I pleasured him with my hands and mouth. I loved giving him head. His dick felt so good in my mouth. I felt like I could suck it forever. He started gyrating in my mouth and I knew he would climax soon. I released his dick from my mouth and slid down a bit so that I was literally under his genitals. The sound Curtis made sounded inhumane when he felt my tongue flick lightly over his anus. I held him in place by his ass cheeks and licked him mercilessly. There's no shame in my game. When it comes to fucking someone I really connect with, I go all out. Curtis was a mass of quivering flesh and had proclaimed his love for me about ten times by the time I finished tossing his salad.

Shivering mightily, Curtis reached for a condom and rolled it on to his trembling cock.

"You're something else..." he whispered.

I merely smiled and turned my back to him, bending over slightly and placing my hands on the edge of the Jacuzzi for support.

Breathing heavily, he positioned himself behind me and inserted his dick slowly with a loud groan. I knew he was marveling at my tightness. Two years without penetration could work wonders for even the most well-used pussy, much less one with a low mileage such as mine. His entry was painful. I could feel my pussy being stretched. But it was sweet pain. It hurt like hell but it felt good.

"Take your time babes...its been awhile...oh my god...it hurts so good..."

He controlled the urge to fuck me like I knew he really wanted to and settled into a nice, easy rhythm. The pain lessened and the pleasure intensified. God I missed having a nice sized dick inside me.

"Oh yeah...that's it...ooohh baby...I love it..." I moaned as I began to thrust my ample ass against him, meeting him stroke for stroke.

I turned my head and looked at him.

"You like my pussy Curtis?"

"I *love* your pussy baby..."

"I'm about to come all over your long dick Curtis...I'm about to drown your cock...don't stop...sweet gentle Jesus... ohhhh"

I came hard. My pussy grabbed his dick and choked it as I gritted my teeth and bathed his dick with my essence.

"Oh god Curtis...mmmm...oh lord..." I felt high. His dick was like potent marijuana. I felt like I was floating in the water instead of standing knee-deep in it.

Curtis started to spank me with each stroke. It stung. I loved it. I felt yet another orgasm approaching.

"No...it's not possible...I just came...Jesus Christ...oh Curtis...fuuuck!"

I shook my head from side to side in disbelief as my pussy exploded in a million tiny pieces. Pleasure like I've never experienced it before held me a willing hostage. I didn't recognize the sounds emanating from my mouth. It sounded like an exotic animal was in the room. Curtis was tearing my back out. Fucking me like he owned my pussy. I didn't want him to come in the condom. I wanted to feel his hot juice all over my face and breasts. I turned my head slightly and looked at him.

His handsome face was a study of blissful concentration. He was watching his dick slide in and out of my tight wetness as my ass jiggled with each stroke.

"Oh god...fuck me Curtis...you feel so good inside me...I want you to come all over me baby...I want to feel your kids trickling down my face..."

That drove him berserk.

He grunted loudly and continuously as he pumped me fast and hard, slapping my ass viciously as he did so. I didn't think it was possible but I felt another orgasm building up. I wondered if I would make it before he climaxed. The race was on. I reached down and rubbed my clit furiously as Curtis drilled me mercilessly. I was at the point of no return when I felt him pull out. He grabbed what he could of my short hair and turned my head to face him. Curtis then ripped the condom from his throbbing shaft and pumped his dick with his free hand. Hot semen flooded my face as I closed my eyes and enjoyed our simultaneous orgasm. I continued to rub my clit as I climaxed. It was glorious.

After our breathtaking sex, we took a shower together, polished off the remainder of the champagne and went to bed. Curtis turned to VH1 Soul and we curled up and watched R&B videos. I could hear Curtis' cell phone ringing several times out in the living room but he didn't get up to answer it.

Janelle woke up at 11. She felt rejuvenated. She padded to the bathroom to pee and freshen up. She called Curtis' mobile three times but he didn't answer. She then called Tiffany. It was Thursday night and she had no intention of staying home. There were several places to go. Tiffany answered on the fourth ring.

"Hey girl," Tiffany said breathlessly. "I just got out of the shower."

"Damn, why are you breathing so hard?" Janelle asked.

Tiffany laughed.

"I ran to answer the phone."

"Your apartment aint that big Tiff...you really need to exercise."

"Whatever," Tiffany snorted. "You plan on going on the road?"

"Yeah," Janelle replied. "Maybe we could pass through Bembe or something."

"Ok, I'm going to get dressed now. Pick me up in half-an-hour."

Janelle wondered where Curtis was as she terminated the call. She had spoken to her brother today and knew that he wouldn't be going to Bembe so it would be cool for her to hang with Curtis without having to make sure she wasn't giving away any clues that they were intimately involved. It was rare that her brother and Curtis wouldn't be hanging together at a party, especially one where they were planning to do some promotions for their own upcoming party so she wanted to take advantage. She called him again and sucked her teeth when the phone rang without an answer. She went to the closet to pick out something to wear. The complex where Curtis lived was only ten minutes away from where Bembe was held so she decided to swing by his apartment if he didn't call her back by the time she picked up Tiffany. She did not want to have to walk around in the crowd looking for Curtis once she got to the party.

***

I yawned and looked at my watch. It was 11:15 p.m. I nudged Curtis. We had both fallen asleep about twenty minutes after we had started watching TV. He didn't budge. I started to suck his exposed right nipple.

That did the trick. He moaned sleepily and opened his eyes. He smiled.

"Ready for round two?"

"I don't think I can take any more tonight baby...I can hardly walk as it is..."

Curtis laughed. He looked at the time. "I have to get ready and go on the road. I have some things to deal with."

"Ok, good. My pussy has fallen in love with your magic stick but she needs to rest now."

He grinned and hopped off the bed, his long dick swinging like a golf club.

I looked up at the TV when he disappeared into the bathroom. They were showing a Beyonce video that I hadn't seen before. She sure was churning them out. This was like her fourth video already and the album had only been out for a month.

***

Cutis thought of Kayla while he took a quick shower. She was very intelligent and fun to be around. She was also extremely sexy. It was hard to believe she was thirty-three. She didn't look a day over twenty-five. Janelle was sexy as hell too but Kayla had

21

an ass that just didn't quit. She was also a freak with a capital F. He was glad he met her.

***

"Sup, you look hot girl, that dress is banging," Tiffany declared when she got into Janelle's black Toyota Rav 4.

"Thanks," Janelle responded as she sped off hurriedly. She was a bit worried that something might be wrong with Curtis. It wasn't like him not to return her calls and she was sure that he wasn't already at Bembe. It was only a few minutes to twelve. She decided she would definitely swing by his apartment.

***

Curtis wrapped himself in a towel and went into the living room to check his mobile. He had missed twenty calls, including four from Janelle. He returned a couple of the calls, including one to Shonda, who was in charge of the crew of girls that would be handing out promotional stuff for him. She assured him that they were all there at Bembe working. He told her he would be there shortly. He decided he would call back Janelle later. He went into the bedroom to get dressed.

***

Janelle got to the apartment complex and honked the horn. A new guard was now on duty but they all knew her car. He opened the gate and waved her through. She tooted her horn in greeting and headed down to Curtis' apartment. His truck was parked in its spot and there was light in the bedroom. The TV was on. *Poor thing must have fallen asleep*, she mused. She passed his truck and was about to reverse into the spot next to it when she realized that a vehicle was there. She parallel parked behind the two vehicles instead and got out.

"Who are we picking up J?" Tiffany asked.

Janelle ignored her as she checked out the vehicle. She didn't recognize it.

Tiffany was bewildered. Janelle was acting really strange. Tiffany wondered who lived at the apartment and why Janelle was so interested in the Toyota Mark 11. Tiffany glanced at the car. Her friend Kayla had one that same colour. She didn't think that was it, though she wasn't sure as she didn't remember Kayla's license plate number. She gasped when Janelle, apparently not getting through to whoever she was calling, stormed to the front door and started banging on it loudly.

***

I was sucking the hell out of Curtis' dick when we heard the banging on the door. He had taken me up on my challenge that I could make him climax in five minutes just by giving him head. Curtis seemed shocked that someone was beating down his door. Instinct told me to get up and get dressed. I got up and he wrapped himself in his towel and went out to investigate muttering "who the fuck could that be?"

"Curtis! Curtis!" I heard an irate female voice begin to shout. I doubled my efforts in getting dressed. I hope this isn't what I think it is. I cannot deal with the drama.

***

What the fuck is Janelle doing here, Curtis thought angrily as he opened the door and stepped outside, closing it behind him.

"Baby, why are you out here acting crazy?" Curtis asked, trying to be calm. "Why didn't you call before coming by? Suppose I wasn't here?"

Janelle's pretty face was flushed and her chest was heaving mightily.

"Why are we outside talking Curtis? And whose car is that in your driveway?" she asked, ignoring his questions.

Tiffany couldn't believe what was happening. So that's the guy that Janelle was seeing. Curtis from Golden Touch Promotions. She knew him. Not personally but she knew who he was. She opened the door and got out of the car. She had to be there for her friend if things got ugly.

"Go home Janelle, I'm about to get dressed. I have some business to take care of on the road."

Janelle lost it. She just knew he had a woman in the house. She tried to push Curtis from in front of the door but he held her easily and told her to chill and stop embarrassing him.

"Why can't I go in the house Curtis? Huh? Why the fuck I have to stand outside *my* man's house to talk to him? That's how you treating me Curtis? Am I not your woman?"

Janelle was crying now.

Curtis couldn't believe this was happening. He was thinking of something to say when Janelle pulled his towel and it crumbled at his feet in a heap. She pushed him aside when he reached down to quickly pick it up.

Damn! Tiffany thought when she saw his dick. *Curtis is blessed!* She stopped lusting and ran inside the house where Janelle had disappeared with Curtis hot on her heels.

***

I was fully dressed and had my pocket book and car keys in hand when a young woman ran into the bedroom. She stopped short when she saw me standing by the bed. She was a pretty little petite thing. She was livid. Her fists were clenched, her eyes screamed murder and her body was taut with anger. This must be the girlfriend that Curtis claimed lived abroad. Men. Why do they have to lie? I would've still fucked him. Just wouldn't have lazed around in his apartment afterwards if I knew his girl lived here and could just show up at his place.

"Look, I am about to leave. Whatever issue you have, it's with Curtis and not with me. Just step aside and allow me to leave peacefully," I said sincerely and calmly. I'm pretty sure I could beat her in a fight but I didn't want to go there. Fighting over a man? Nope, not my style. Curtis came to a screeching halt behind her. He looked angry, bewildered and apologetic at the same time. I'm guessing it's the first time he has been caught. I thought of the two times I had caught Ralston, my ex. Now *I* was the other woman. Aint that a bitch. Someone else ran into the bedroom. Oh my God.

"Tiffany!" I couldn't believe it. What was Tiff doing here?

"Fucking hell! Kayla? What yuh doing here wid de people dem man?" Tiffany said in shock. "I thought yuh was a *christian* now."

That made me mad. She's supposed to be my best friend even though we haven't hung out in awhile. Disloyal bitch.

I ignored her and said to Curtis, "Control your girlfriend. I'm leaving now."

"You little slut," the girlfriend snarled. "You think that you can just come in here and fuck my man and walk out? Eeeh gal?"

With that she pounced. I was forced to defend myself. I dropped my pocketbook and keys as I tried to push her off me. She would not be deterred and managed to give me a nasty scratch to the face. She drew blood. That did it. I punched her in the neck and followed that up with two brutal slaps to the face. I was about to slap her again when I felt a hard punch to my right ear. It hurt like hell but it hurt even more to know that Tiffany, my long time best friend, had attacked me for a bitch I'm sure she had only recently met. The shock distracted me long enough for the girlfriend to inflict a painful bite on my arm. I screamed. Tiffany started raining blows to my head, shouting that I tricked her, and that it was because I wanted time to whore down the place why I stopped hanging with her and lied that I was now into the church. Tiffany was almost as strong as I was and the girlfriend attacked me with renewed vigour when she realized that she had help. I didn't stand a chance. The two women beat the hell out of me as I tried valiantly to ward them off. Curtis was nowhere in sight.

If only I had torn up his business card.

Decisions. It's amazing how they shape your life.

The Fan

The noise in the club was deafening. The club was packed; bursting at the seams with a close to equal mix of enthralled young women and men, raucously singing and rapping along to Money XL, the latest rapper to blow up in the United States. His unique sing-song flow, catchy hooks and hardcore lyrics, had landed him two top ten singles on the billboard charts and a growing legion of fans worldwide. Born in a public hospital in the Bronx to Jamaican immigrants, this was his first time in Jamaica and he was having a blast. He had been pleasantly surprised to discover that the crowd knew the words to all his songs. They had embraced and claimed him as their own. Jamaica had spawned many musical stars, but this was their first hip hop star. Money XL walked to the edge of the stage, took off his tank top, and threw it in the frenzied crowd as he launched into his soon to be released third single. There was a brief scuffle as four women fought for the right to own an article of Money XL's clothing. They ended up ripping it shreds.

Mindy admired his chiseled, heavily-tattooed physique from her vantage point directly in front of the stage. She had read in an article that he had served twenty months in jail for gun possession. Apparently he had put the time to good use. He had hit the streets running upon his release. Armed with a notebook of hits, a body to die for and street credibility from his stint in jail, he had become a force to reckon with in just one short year. She had arrived at the club two and a half hours before showtime just to ensure that she would be close to the stage. She had watched footage of some of his shows and he always selected an attractive woman from the audience to come on to the stage when he performed *I need a girl*, his biggest hit to date. She was confident she would be selected. Mindy looked hot. And available. Tight, short designer dress showing off her luscious ass and large, firm breasts. Six-inch-come-fuck-me stilettos. Hair well done. Flawless make-up. She looked around at the other women in close proximity. Some of them were attractive but there was no doubt in her mind that when Money XL laid eyes on her she would be the one on that stage. From what she had seen on the tapes she watched, the woman selected was allowed to remain onstage for the rest of the show.

Mindy was very excited. She had an extraordinary crush on the ruggedly handsome entertainer. She had dreamt about meeting him and fucking his brains out on many occasions. The dreams had intensified when she heard that he was going to perform in Jamaica. She had been at her desk typing up her weekly sales report when she heard the ad on the radio. She had become wet instantly. Though she was in a committed three year relationship, Mindy could not allow this opportunity to pass her by. How many people really got the chance to live out their ultimate fantasy? She had used her lunch time the following day to go to one of the three designated ticket locations to purchase her ticket. Tickets were limited as the venue could only accommodate 1000 people.

Mindy had confided in Sharlene, her best friend, about her intense crush on the rap star. What she didn't tell Sharlene was that she actually planned to fuck him. Sharlene and the other two girls they regularly hung out with were also at the show, but they were upstairs to the right of the stage as their boyfriends did not want to be so close to the action. Ethan, her boyfriend, did not like hip hop – he was more into R&B and old school reggae – so he was shooting pool at his usual hang-out spot.

Mindy felt her LG Chocolate vibrating in her pocketbook. She managed to tear her eyes away from the stage long enough to remove the phone and check who was trying to reach her. It was a text message from Sharlene asking if she was ok. She replied quickly that she was fine and that she would see them outside after the show. Her heart beat accelerated as she placed the phone back into her pocket book and looked up on the stage. Money XL was now asking the ladies in the audience if they knew what time it was as he walked teasingly up to the very edge of the stage, his two stone-faced bodyguards vigilant on either side of him. The deafening screams that answered his question told him that they did indeed. It was time. The moment she had been waiting for. Her date with destiny. Mindy remained quiet amidst the screaming throng around her and kept her eyes squarely on Money XL. The look on her face was one of studied disinterest.

Money XL smiled as he surveyed the women that were closest to the stage. They were all waving and yelling "Pick me!" All except one. The short-haired cutie with the large breasts was watching him with a look that suggested she couldn't care less whether he chose her or not. He gave her a piercing look and pointed at her.

He whispered something to one of his bodyguards who gestured at Mindy for her to walk around to the right of the stage. Mindy had dreamt of this moment. Wanted it to happen. Expected it to happen. But now that it was actually happening, it felt surreal. She was sure she could hear her heart pounding over the noise in the club. She smiled at the envious looks thrown her way by the other women as she made her way to the stage.

"But wait! Nuh Mindy dat?" Sharlene squealed rhetorically as she looked at the sexy female being escorted onto the stage by the burly bodyguard.

"She same one," her boyfriend, Clive, replied. The group of four watched excitedly as Mindy strutted towards Money XL in the middle of the stage. The rap star smiled and held her hand as the stage went dark. A single spotlight then shone on the couple as the infectious beat for the song he was about to do came on.

Mindy smiled nervously as she reveled in the moment. She was about to be serenaded by the hottest rapper in the world. She looked up in his face as he launched into the intro for the song. He was even more handsome in person: long curly cornrows, full lips, bushy eyebrows over piercing hooded eyes, high cheekbones and a pair of dimples that softened his ruggedness when he smiled. Oftentimes with celebrities, it was the other way around. They looked fabulous in glossy magazine pictures and on TV, but looked ordinary and average in person. Mindy gasped as he pulled her up against him suddenly and started to gyrate sensuously. Mindy boldly caressed his muscular chest as she moved in sync with him. Though the women in the audience were screaming at the top of their lungs, Mindy felt as though they were alone in the venue. The way he looked deeply in her eyes as he rapped and held her close as he moved his pelvis against hers, made her hot all over. She could feel his hardness pressing into her groin and she smiled. Now she knew what the XL in his name was for.

He spun her around and bent her over much to the delight of the crowd. Mindy turned her head and gave him a come-hither look as she ground her ample ass expertly on his pelvis. She was far too excited and aroused to be embarrassed by their raunchy display on stage. The song ended and Money XL pulled her to him and held her for a moment.

"Private after-party at the Presidential Suite at the Matarese," he whispered, giving Mindy's ear a quick flick of his tongue. With that he handed her off to one of his bodyguards and turned his attention to the crowd. She felt like she was walking on water as she made her way backstage.

"One more joint people and then it's party time!" Money XL yelled to thunderous applause as he closed what had been a rapturous performance. Two popular local DJs were on hand to play music after the show ended.

Mindy stood to the rear of the stage with Money XL's management and various hangers-on. A very attractive, exotic-looking woman stared her down for a few seconds. Mindy ignored her. Ovbiously she was connected to Money XL. Maybe one of his women. *You can have him sweetheart,* Mindy mused. *I'm just here for the experience.*

***

Ethan checked the time. It was now 1a.m. The sports bar was thinning out now, only he and five other people were still there. He wondered if the show was over. He was far from sleepy and felt like seeing Mindy tonight. He decided to play one more game and then swing by the venue and call her when he was outside.

***

Money XL ran along the length of the edge of the stage and touched as many people as he could before shouting "I love you Jamaica!" and exited the stage with everyone in tow. Mindy, unsure of what to do, followed everyone else into the hallway that led to the dressing room area. Members of Money XL's entourage were in the hallway drinking, smoking and talking to some attractive scantily clad women. Mindy was certain they were around there for the same reason she was. Damn groupies. Mindy didn't consider herself a groupie. Groupies would fuck any celebrity they could get their manicured claws on. She was simply trying to fulfill her ultimate fantasy. Did that make her a groupie? No, she didn't think so. She walked slowly but confidently down the hall, making her way through the crowd. When she got to the end of the hallway, the bodyguard that had escorted her onstage was sitting on a chair conversing with two men.

He stopped in the middle of his sentence and looked up at her with a smirk. He waited for her to speak. Mindy felt weird standing there with the three men undressing her with their eyes. They all knew what she wanted. She cleared her throat nervously.

"Umm...Money XL invited me to the after-party at the Matarese...will I be riding with him there?"

The bodyguard stroked his goatee.

"I don't know anything about that shorty," he said in an American accent, his beady eyes now taking in the generous amount of cleavage on display.

"But he told me that right after we finished dancing...just go and ask him," Mindy replied with annoyance. She did not reach this far to let some stupid oversized bodyguard stop her now.

The man snorted. "I've heard that story about ten times tonight shorty...that after-party is really exclusive...people will say anything to get to party with the hottest rapper in the game."

"So you're not going to ask him?" Mindy was incredulous. She looked beyond the three men. There were two rooms behind them. The doors were closed. The sign on one door indicated it was a bathroom so Mindy surmised that the other must be the dressing room. The light was on and she could hear voices and laughter.

The bodyguard grinned.

"How badly do you want to hang with Money XL tonight?" he asked, looking directly in her eyes.

Mindy maintained eye contact but didn't answer. She wasn't stupid. She knew where this going. But could she?

The bodyguard pressed on. "A lot of women are trying to get with him tonight but only one will get lucky...if you play your cards right that lucky woman will be you..."

Fucking hell, Mindy thought. *How badly do I want this?* She remembered being on stage with Money XL and feeling his hard dick pressing against her pelvis...remembered how he flicked his tongue against her ear...his smell...his muscular frame...her dreams...

Mindy sighed. She knew there was no way she was going to turn back now and wonder what if for the rest of her life. She just had to get with Money XL. She was obsessed with him.

"What do I have to do?" Mindy asked, with a resigned expression.

The bodyguard grinned. "You seem to be a nice girl shorty... so I'll make it easy on you...you'll only have to do me."

Mindy snorted. "If I'm so nice why don't you just let us skip this segment and take me to Money XL?"

"Shorty, aint no way in hell I'm passing up the opportunity to tap that ass...let's go."

The other two men laughed as Mindy followed the bodyguard into the bathroom.

"Damn...she's sexy as hell son," the skinny one with the dreads said to his cousin. "Big Mike should share the wealth...that's fucked up. Selfish motherfucker."

"Word," his cousin agreed as he lit up a blunt. He didn't mind too much though. There'd be a lot of groupies at the after-party and he was positive he would get some pussy. He checked the time. It was 1:45 a.m. He figured they would be rolling out to the hotel soon.

<hr/>

"Gimme some head," Big Mike instructed, as he leaned against the large double sink and took out his half-erect dick.

Mindy wondered absently how many women his fat ass had screwed because he was a direct link to Money XL. Probably hundreds.

"Put on a condom," Mindy told him in a no nonsense tone.

"Hell no...not until I'm ready to fuck," Big Mike said. "I want to *feel* those juicy lips of yours."

"Look, I give a hell of a blow job. Trust me...you won't even remember that you have on a rubber. Please. Just put a condom on that big juicy dick and let me do my thing," she cooed, stroking his ego. She didn't want him to give her an ultimatum.

"Alright shorty," Big Mike agreed grudgingly and took out a condom. "They don't call me Big Mike for nothin'."

Whatever, Mindy thought inwardly. His dick was short and stubby. It had a little girth but nothing to write home about. He was really big everywhere except where it mattered most. She figured he weighed at least two hundred and eighty pounds and he was over six feet tall. She was just grateful that he had complied. Mindy stroked his dick and he became fully erect. Breathing heavily, he rolled on the condom and Mindy squatted in front of him. She took him in her mouth slowly, sucking gently on the tip before working her way down to the base. Big Mike moaned loudly as Mindy licked, sucked and stroked his turgid cock while fondling his balls.

"Mmmmm....you are good...damn shorty...fuck...oh shit..."

Mindy pumped his cock aggressively as she tried to make him come quickly. She did not want him to penetrate her.

Big Mike seemed to read her mind.

"Oh shit...stop...stop...stop!" he said forcefully.

Mindy released his trembling dick and stood up. She almost had him. At least he wouldn't last long once he got inside her.

Big Mike turned her around and bent her over the sink. He hiked up her dress and spread her legs. She wasn't wearing any panties. He couldn't help but stop and admire her body. This was one fine, sexy Jamaican woman. Strong shapely legs, rich caramel skin and an ass that could only have been designed by a man. Big Mike couldn't resist. He knelt down between her legs and spread her ass cheeks. He licked around her anus and then he stuck his tongue inside as far as it would go.

Mindy was shocked. Big Mike was a mega freak! He moaned and stroked his dick as he licked her ass enthusiastically.

"You like that shorty....huh...you like the way I'm tossing your salad...huh...mmmm..."

She had never experienced it before and the feeling was indescribable. She moaned involuntarily as he reamed her virgin anus with his tongue. *I'll never forget this moment*, Mindy mused with her eyes tightly closed as she enjoyed the sensations wracking her voluptuous body, *when Money XL's 280 lb gorilla of a bodyguard licked and sucked my asshole in the bathroom of Club Mars like it was the sweetest tasting candy on earth.*

***

Ethan pulled up across the street from Club Mars at 2 p.m. He had called Mindy's cell phone twice on his way from the sports bar but it rang out to voicemail both times. He saw Tristan, one of his co-workers that he was close to at the office, coming across the street with Doreen, his girlfriend, in tow. Ethan smiled to himself. Those two were something else. Every week they broke up. And every week they got back together. Doreen was a big flirt and it always caused them to have a fight. Ethan was glad he didn't have those issues with Mindy. As sexy as Mindy was, she had only eyes for him and was very committed to the relationship. They had been together for three years and Ethan figured that he would propose to her when it got to the five year mark.

Tristan spotted him and came over to his car. Ethan put the car in park and came out. The two men knocked fists in greeting.

"Yo, the show did wicked!" Tristan enthused as Ethan nodded a greeting to Doreen, who was scowling. "Money XL ah de boss!"

Guess they just had another argument, he mused.

"Ok, cool," Ethan commented. "It finish long time?"

"Nuh really...about forty-five minutes ago. Plenty people still inside...DJ Fire playing right now," Tristan said.

"Rassclaat!" Tristan then exclaimed. "Almost forget to tell yuh...yuh girl was onstage a wine up pon Money XL!"

"What!" Ethan said in surprise. Mindy on stage?

"Yeah man...him pick her out of the audience fi serenade pon stage," Tristan said, adding, "trust mi...she look like she did ah really enjoy herself..."

Ethan leaned against the car. Why would Mindy do something like that? Go on stage to cavort with that misogynistic rapper?

"Yuh shoulda see her outfit," Doreen chimed in, "not even my dress nuh short so..."

Ethan couldn't believe what he was hearing. Doreen's dress barely covered her ass. Surely she was exaggerating. He had never seen Mindy wear anything that short, except around the house.

"Alright then Ethan, see you on Monday," Tristan told him as he and Doreen left and made their way down the street to catch a cab home. Ethan could only manage a nod. He whipped out his phone to call Mindy again.

* * *

Big Mike finally ceased his oral assault on Mindy's booty and entered her from behind with a hard thrust. Mindy placed her left leg on top of the sink to give him better access. All the better for him to climax quickly. She maintained eye contact with him through the mirror above the sink. Big Mike's face was a canvas of sweaty bliss. He gritted his teeth and his gold tooth glistened in the lighting as he tried unsuccessfully to hold back his orgasm.

"Oh shit shorty...daddy's about to blow...oh god...damn this some good ass pussy...arrrgghhh..."

Big Mike's hefty frame shook mightily as he blew his wad with much fanfare.

He collapsed on Mindy, nearly breaking her back.

"Hey! Ease up man!" Mindy exclaimed. "You must be trying to kill me!"

"My bad shorty," Big Mike apologized breathlessly. "That shit was so good my knees just gave way."

Mindy tried hard to suppress a grin. This night had been some experience and the best was still to come.

Mindy retrieved her make up kit from her pocket book and started to freshen up.

"Where Big Mike at?" they both heard a voice say out in the hall way. Money XL.

"Oh shit," Big Mike mumbled as he pulled his zipper up and went out into the hallway.

"Sup boss," Big Mike said, as he quickly closed the bathroom door behind him.

"Where's the honey dip that I had on stage with me? Didn't I tell your fat ass to make sure that she was comfortable until I'm ready to go to the hotel?" Money XL asked, as he checked his messages on his Apple iPhone.

Mindy froze by the sink where she had been applying some blush to her cheeks. That fucking bastard! She couldn't believe the piece of shit had tricked her like that. She restrained herself from going out into the hallway. She had a gut feeling that Money XL would not touch her with a long stick if he knew that Big Mike had had sex with her. She seethed in silence and continued to freshen up as she listened to their conversation.

"Yeah...she...ummm...she's somewhere up by the hallway entrance," Big Mike stammered, ignoring the look of incredulity on the faces of the two guys that had been chilling with him when Mindy showed up. Big Mike cursed inwardly. He would have to give them some money or something for them not to tell Money XL what really happened. Money XL would fire him immediately. He didn't tolerate his employees or anyone from his entourage not following his instructions.

"You think that's what the fuck I meant when I said to make sure she was comfortable? To have her standing out in the hallway with those knuckleheads?" Money XL glared at him. "I'm just about ready to roll out. Get the girl, and let everyone know we're ready."

With that he went back inside the dressing room to finish talking with a popular Jamaican singer who wanted to do a remix with him. The singer had been invited to the after-party but Money XL preferred to discuss business now as he just planned to have fun at the party.

Ethan slammed his flip phone shut in annoyance. He wasn't getting through to Mindy. He decided to just wait outside until she exited the club. More people were streaming out of the club and he spotted Mindy's group of friends. She was not with them.

"Sharlene!" Ethan shouted, and waved her over. She waved back and they all crossed the street and came over to him. He greeted everyone and asked Sharlene for Mindy.

"Last I saw her she was chilling backstage," Sharlene told him. "She was supposed to meet up back with us outside after the show but I've been texting and calling her without a response. Seems like her phone is off."

"I heard she was on the stage carrying on badly with that rapper," Ethan said, adding, "how come she wasn't hanging with you guys inside anyway?"

"Well...she wanted to be close to the stage but we wanted to watch the show from the balcony so we had split up," Sharlene explained.

<hr/>

"Damn Big Mike...you done fucked up son," Scrappy, the skinny one with the dreads said when Money XL was out of ear shot. "If the boss finds out..."

"Be cool yo," Big Mike snarled. "I'm gonna make it worth your while. Just chill."

"We want two grand each or we're telling," Scrappy promptly announced.

Mindy came out of the bathroom and slapped Big Mike in the face before he could react to Scrappy's demands.

"You piece of shit," she said to him angrily. "Damn gorilla...is that the only way you can get pussy? You pathetic asshole!"

"You aint shit but a groupie. Fuck you!" Big Mike retorted, bristling from her insults and embarrassed by the slap.

"Don't worry yourself...you'll get what's coming to you soon enough," Mindy told him with a disgusted look.

They became quiet as the door of the dressing room opened and Money XL came out along with the singer, a lanky fellow who looked more like an athlete than an entertainer, and the exotic-looking woman that Mindy had noticed while waiting backstage.

Money XL smiled at Mindy as he walked by, still in conversation with the singer.

When they got to the door leading back out to the club, the promoter came over to have a quick word with Money XL and to organize an escort for him to exit the club.

Flanked by his bodyguards and three members of the club's security team, Money XL quickly made his way through the club with his entourage, and headed towards the exit. Mindy felt like a celebrity as she made her way out behind him. Everyone was watching them. When they got outside, two stretch Cadillac limousines, two Chevy Suburbans and a Dodge Magnum were waiting to take them to the hotel. Mindy was ushered into the limo that was transporting Money XL. She thought she heard someone shouting her name when she was getting into the vehicle but she didn't look in the direction of the voice.

"Mindy!" Ethan shouted as he ran across the street towards the car he had seen her get in. Sharlene and the others had just walked off when he looked across the street and saw Money XL and his entourage exiting the club. He had almost fainted when he saw Mindy, looking sexier than ever, going into the limo with the rap star.

The limo they were in was in the middle of the five vehicle convoy and he got to it just as they were about to move off. The tinted window seemed to mock him silently as he knocked on it shouting Mindy's name. Where the hell did she think she was going with Money XL?

"Who is this asshole?" Money XL asked no one in particular as the limo pulled off slowly. A policeman had stopped the flow of traffic coming down the hip strip to allow the convoy to proceed. "Does anyone know him?"

39

"Probably just a crazed fan seeking an autograph or some shit," Future, Money XL's road manager replied.

"Yeah, I guess," Money XL agreed, as he gestured that he wanted something to drink. Mindy watched as the exotic-looking woman who apparently never left his side poured him a shot of Hennessey. Mindy felt a twinge of guilt as she watched Ethan's bewildered and angry face through the window. She was sorry he saw her get into the limo but there was nothing she could do about it. As far as she was concerned, she was on a date with destiny. Ethan would eventually get over it. She knew how much he loved her. Mindy felt hot and bothered as she wondered if Money XL was watching her. She was seated directly across from him but he had slipped on a pair of very dark oversized Cartier shades upon exiting the club, so she couldn't see his eyes. He probably was. There was a very generous amount of her thick, smooth thighs on display. Mindy sighed as she accepted a glass of champagne from Future, who was pouring drinks for everyone else in the limo. Mindy was a bundle of pent up lust when the limo came to a stop. They had arrived at the hotel.

<hr />

Ethan walked dejectedly back to his car with the laughter of those who had witnessed what just happened ringing in his ears, wishing this night was simply a bad dream and he would wake up musing at the craziness he had just dreamt. Alas, it was all too real. His girlfriend had just ignored him and left in a limousine with a famous rapper. That could only mean one thing. He could feel a migraine coming on as he tried to wrap his head around the situation. He couldn't believe Mindy would embarrass and disrespect him like that. He couldn't believe that she would throw away everything they had together and all their future plans for a one night stand with a celebrity. He just couldn't believe it. How was he going to sleep tonight?

<hr />

It was Mindy's first time at the Matarese. It was Kingston's largest and swankiest hotel, and its class was evident from the moment one stepped into the expansive lobby. Tastefully and expensively decorated in rich, dark hues with a knowledgeable and courteous staff; and with a complex that housed a state of the art gym, an internet café, a sports bar, an award-winning restaurant and a clothing store, it was *the* place that celebrities stayed when they traveled to Kingston. The lobby was buzzing with activity and Money XL stopped to chat for a few minutes with a NBA player who was hosting a three day basketball clinic in Kingston. The entourage of twenty eight people then made their way to the 10th floor along with the thirty invited guests who were milling about in the lobby, waiting for Money XL to arrive. Money XL had rented the entire top floor of that section of the hotel for his three day stay; fifteen rooms in all plus the Presidential Suite.

Money XL's DJ quickly set up his state of the art turntables, and with the food and liquor already laid out, the party started instantly. Mindy watched as Money XL disappeared into the hallway leading to the bedroom accompanied by the exotic-looking woman who seemed to be his second skin. She assumed he was going to freshen up. A waiter approached her with a tray filled with champagne and she accepted a glass. Mindy sipped and rocked to the beat of Rhianna's latest hit as she looked around the jampacked suite. She recognized a few local celebrities in the mix. She saw a well-known party promoter, three models, a popular track & field star, and the current 'it' reggae artiste who had a huge crossover hit that was making waves in the United States and the United Kingdom. She watched as Future, Money XL's road manager swapped saliva freely with a voluptuous light-skinned girl who didn't look a day over eighteen. Everyone was drinking and having a good time. The scent of pungent marijuana and expensive colognes and perfumes permeated the air-conditioned room. Some people were also out on the large balcony which provided a lovely view of the hilly residential area of Kingston's Beverly Hills.

A man who identified himself as Money XL's best friend struck up a conversation with Mindy and she listened to amusing anecdotes – greatly exaggerated she was sure – of his and Money XL's childhood experiences. She was on her third glass of bubbly when Money XL emerged from the bedroom with the exotic-looking woman in tow. He was wearing a black Ed Hardy wife-beater with Evisu shorts and a pair of custom-made, black, suede Air Force Ones. He was draped in platinum jewellery. She was wearing a Christian Dior shorts set and stilettos. Mindy had to admit to herself that she was one of the most beautiful women she had ever seen in person. Exquisite even.

Money XL gave her a smile as he made his way through the crowd meeting and greeting his guests. He had yet to speak to Mindy since he whispered in her ear onstage. She was certain she would collapse from anxiety any minute now. She tried to relax and enjoy herself, knowing he would either come to her or send for her in due time. It was difficult though. All she could think of was what it would be like to have Money XL inside her. Money XL's alleged best friend was still by her side chatting up a storm but she barely heard a word he said since Money XL entered the room.

<hr/>

Forty-five minutes had passed since Ethan saw the love of his life get into the limo with the rap star. He was still standing by his car in a daze when he overheard the conversation of a raucous group of three men and two women as they walked by. One of the women was commenting that it was a pity that they were not able to go to the after party at the Matarese as it was bound to be off the chain. She proceeded to demonstrate to her friends the 'wine' that she would use to make Money XL fall in love and take her back to the US with him. The group laughed loudly at her lewd antics. That woke Ethan out of his stupor. He hopped in his car and drove off. He decided he would try to get into the party and if that wasn't possible, wait in the lobby until Mindy showed up. He just couldn't go home without confronting her.

Mindy, though enjoying the vibe and the lustful looks she was getting from several of the men, was starting to think that Money XL was taking too long to get the ball rolling. She wondered if he didn't hear her pussy calling him. An hour had passed since he made his entrance in the party, and having consumed four glasses of champagne, and observing some risqué behaviour on the part of some of the guests, Mindy was ready for action. The last time she glimpsed him he had been in a corner dancing with two women and smoking a blunt. She glanced over there. Different people now occupied that spot. Mindy scanned the room furtively. Money XL was nowhere to be seen. She hoped he hadn't taken those two girls to his room. She could feel her fantasy slipping away. Maybe he wasn't interested anymore. There were so many attractive women at the party and he could have almost any one of them he desired, maybe he had seen one that had knocked her out of his consciousness. Her confidence now shaken, Mindy gestured to the waiter to bring her another glass of champagne. She took the glass and took a big sip as she contemplated what to do.

"Come with me," a sultry voice instructed in her right ear. Mindy was startled. She was so distraught that she hadn't even noticed that anyone had come up to her. It was the exotic-looking woman. She stepped off without a backward glance, confident that Mindy would do her bidding. Now giddy with renewed excitement, Mindy quickly followed her into the small passageway that led to the bedroom. Big Mike and another one of Money XL's bodyguards were stationed a few feet away from the bedroom door. Mindy treated Big Mike to a dirty look as she strutted past him. The woman opened the door and stepped aside, allowing Mindy to go in. She gasped at the sight on the large bed.

* * *

Ethan finally found a parking spot after circling the large parking lot several times. A red sports car drove out and he quickly parked in the vacant spot, narrowly edging out a large black Ford F150 that tried to intimidate him. On another day, it would have probably worked, but today was not the day for Ethan to be fucked with. He hurried down to the entrance of the hotel and entered the lobby. Ethan was surprised at the level of activity in the lobby at that hour in the morning. The place was filled with people. He went over to the desk to speak with one of the clerks.

"Good morning," Ethan said. "Which floor is Money XL's party being held?"

The clerk looked him up and down and snickered. "It doesn't matter which floor the party is being held...you can't go up there."

Ethan felt like punching him in the face.

"Look at all those beautiful women who weren't allowed up there," the clerk continued, gesturing behind Ethan at a group of about fifteen attractive, scantily clad women. "What makes you think you would be allowed?"

Ethan sucked his teeth and went over to the small bar at the far end of the lobby. He ordered a drink and stood in a corner. He would wait right there until Mindy came downstairs.

* * *

Money XL was sitting up in the bed, smoking a blunt and drinking Cristal straight from the bottle. He had on a black silk robe. It was open; exposing one of the biggest dicks Mindy had ever laid eyes upon. The term 'third leg' was never more apt. Mindy was yet to move from where she stood when she entered the room. She stood transfixed with her eyes rooted at his genitals. She simply couldn't believe her eyes. It seemed to be at least a foot long and it looked extremely thick and heavy. It was a bulging monster that was waiting to put a hurting on somebody. That somebody was her. Mindy swallowed. She had known that he was well endowed from their antics on the stage but this was ridiculous. The woman had closed the door and was standing directly behind

Mindy. She pulled the zipper on Mindy's dress and slipped it to the floor. Money XL nodded appreciatively at the sight of Mindy's nude body. She was something special.

Mindy still did not move. She watched in awe as the python between Money XL's legs rose slowly at the sight of her naked body. It excited her that she turned him on so easily. Just by standing there. She was extremely wet and her pussy pulsed in sync with her accelerated heart beat. The woman undressed herself quickly and started to kiss Mindy all over her back. Mindy, though she had never been with a woman before, was adventurous by nature and savoured the unfamiliar sensations of a woman's touch. She moaned when she felt the woman's soft hands massaging her ample breasts. Mindy whimpered as the woman's tongue slivered along the small of her back as she reached between her legs and cupped her sarcoid mound. She spread Mindy's legs and her tongue snaked into Mindy's wetness as she started to eat her out from behind.

"Oh god...oh god...oh god..." Mindy groaned like a wounded animal as all her pent up lust erupted in a quick, unexpected, explosive climax. There was no familiar buildup, just an intense burst of pleasure that made her body quiver uncontrollably. She managed to open her eyes and look at Money XL. He was watching them intensely. The woman stood up and kissed Mindy on the mouth. Mindy tasted herself as she enjoyed her first kiss with a woman. It was a soft, warm, passionate kiss. Strangely erotic and quite different from kissing a man. They hugged each other tightly as Mindy moaned and deepened the kiss even more, cupping the woman's head as their tongues danced with fiery desire.

Mindy then lowered her head and took one of the woman's succulent breasts in her mouth. She could feel the nipple hardening. The woman moaned and spread her legs, inviting Mindy to play with her pussy. Mindy slipped a finger in, then two, and worked them in and out of the woman's wetness in a see-saw motion. Whenever Mindy masturbated, this was how she quickly brought herself to climax. It excited her to see that it worked on the woman as well. She grabbed a fistful of Mindy's short hair and screamed loudly as she came all over Mindy's nimble fingers. Still moaning, she removed Mindy's fingers and licked them sensuously, enjoying the taste of her own secretions. It was now time for the main event.

The two women slowly joined Money XL on the king-sized bed. They went on either side of him. Mindy was beside herself with excitement and unbridled lust. This was the moment she had been waiting for. While the other woman ran her lips and tongue along the length of his massive tool, Mindy claimed his lips in a searching, searing kiss that spoke volumes of her desire for him. Money XL groaned in her mouth. He could *feel* the extent of her heat and passion. He returned her kiss ardently, exploring her mouth and sucking on her lips as he caressed her breasts. Mindy then started sucking and nibbling her way down his muscular body. She paid special attentions to his nipples, alternating between biting them roughly and licking them gently. Money XL howled in pleasure when Mindy's mouth joined the other woman's on his genitals. Mindy could hardly get it in her mouth. She concentrated on the head, running her tongue over the slit while she stroked him with both hands. Sweet Jesus, Mindy mused, his dick is so fucking *hard*. She wanted him inside her. Now.

Apparently Money XL was ready too. There was a pack of condoms beside him on the bed and he extracted one and handed it to the woman. She unwrapped it and used her mouth to skillfully roll the condom on to his dick.

"Oh god Karel..." Money XL moaned as he ran his fingers through her hair.

Karel...so that's her name, Mindy mused as she hoisted herself over Money XL and slowly slid down his shaft, whimpering with her eyes tightly closed as she did so.

She sat still when he was fully embedded. She opened her eyes and looked down on him as she savoured the feeling of his gargantuan manhood inside her. She still couldn't believe she was in the Presidential Suite at the Matarese hotel sitting on Money XL's dick. She started to bounce up and down his long shaft slowly, gasping when it reached spots she had no idea were there.

"You like her pussy baby?" Karel asked as she caressed Money XL's chest lovingly. She had met him at a mall in London's West End two months ago where she had worked as a clerk in a high-end designer store. Bowled over by her beauty, Money XL had stayed an extra two days to convince her to go back with him to New York. To the dismay of her family, she left everything behind and went with Money XL. He treated her well and as she was bi-sexual and unaffected by his wild ways, as far as she was concerned, it was the best decision she had made in her twenty two years. It was a fun, glamorous life and she loved every minute of it.

"Fuck yeah...she's so tight...and juicy..." Money XL breathed as he held Mindy's ass in mid air and started thrusting upwards.

"Oh god...bloodclaaat...fuck me...mmmmm...oh rass..." Mindy groaned as the object of her ultimate fantasy fucked her like there was no tomorrow.

"Bumbo...I feel it in my brain!" Mindy shouted as she felt her climax approaching. "Don't stop! Give it to me! Fuck! Ohhhh!"

She shook violently and clenched her buttocks tightly, choking his dick as her orgasm rocked her to the core.

"Sweet baby Jesus..."Mindy murmured blasphemously as she collapsed on Money XL's broad, muscular chest, spent from the intensity of it all.

Money XL then flipped Mindy over onto her back and placed her legs on his shoulder.

"Mmmm...you're stretching the shit outta me...fuck..." she groaned as Money XL gave her long, deep strokes with his impressive tool.

Karel then squatted over Mondy's mouth and Mindy licked her gaping sex while she moaned loudly and squeezed her nipples.

"Fuck me...oh yes...I love it...XL...your dick feels so fucking good..." Mindy said just before Karel climaxed and sat down, covering Mindy's mouth with her gushing pussy. Equal to the task,

Mindy sucked and swallowed everything Karel had to offer until she got up abruptly, her nerves frayed.

They then switched positions and Mindy scrambled to the edge of the bed and tucked her ankles behind her ears, allowing Karel to make an all-you- can-eat-buffet of her pussy. Money XL then ripped off the condom and entered Karel from behind. He fucked her hard and fast, making it impossible for her to concentrate on eating Mindy.

"Oh god baby...just like that baby...you know this is your pussy...fuck it baby!" Karel urged Money XL through clenched teeth as Mindy, immensely turned on by the sight of Karel's petite frame taking such a hard pounding from Money XL, played with her clit furiously as she aimed for her third orgasm.

"Give me that juice baby...fill me with your seed baby...come for me baby...wet it up baby..." Karel coaxed as Money XL groaned loudly and began to fuck her so powerfully that she toppled on top of Mindy who still managed to continue stroking her clit. She was almost there.

What happened next, Mindy would never forget as long she lived.

Ethan was so deep in thought that he didn't even realize that someone was talking to him.

"Sir!" the large, serious looking security guard said in a loud hiss, waking Ethan from his reverie.

"What?" Ethan demanded. He had a massive headache and he was filled with anguish and tension. He had no desire to speak to anyone. All he wanted was to see Mindy come out of one of those elevators.

"I have a complaint from a group of ladies that you have been staring at them with a crazed expression for the past two hours," the security guy told him. Ethan looked beyond the security guard at a group of women sitting a few meters away. One of them shot him a dirty look. "Freak!" he heard her mutter as the group laughed. Ethan imagined taking the cigarette she was smoking and putting it out on the tip of that long, aristocratic nose of hers.

"Mi not even notice the bitch them," Ethan snarled dismissively, sucking his teeth.

"I'm going to have to ask you to leave the premises sir," the security guard informed him in a tone which suggested that it wasn't really a request. "It's clear that you have no business here and the Materese is not a place for loiterers."

"I'm waiting on someone," Ethan replied firmly, looking him square in the face.

The security guard took that as a challenge and grabbed Ethan by his right hand, twisting it painfully. Another security guard came over and they lifted Ethan unceremoniously by the waist of his jeans and removed him from the lobby.

Ethan struggled and was rewarded with three hard punches to his side and stomach when they got outside.

"Hey bwoy, yuh drive?" one of the security guards asked derisively.

Doubled over in pain and coughing, Ethan nodded.

"Go get yuh vehicle and leave the bloodclaat premises!" the guard told him, giving him a hard kick to the ass for good measure. Ethan fell on his face, bruising his chin.

"He was planning to rape a woman inside," one of the guards explained to two onlookers who had come up on the scene.

"Oh," the man said, nodding his head in understanding as he took his girlfriend's hand and made his way to the lobby.

Embarrassed, angry and hurting, Ethan got up slowly and made his way to the parking lot to retrieve his vehicle. In four crazy hours his life just didn't make any sense any more. The woman he loved was in a hotel suite getting fucked by a celebrity while he was downstairs getting fucked up by a couple of over zealous security guards. Life could certainly be a menstruating bitch sometimes.

All three of them climaxed simultaneously.

"Fucking hell I'm coming!" Karel announced loudly in her British accent as she sank her teeth in Mindy's neck, giving her a painful hicky as her petite frame convulsed with pleasure.

Mindy screamed from the pain of Karel's vicious love bite and the force of her own intense climax, enhanced by the incredible blend of pain and pleasure.

"Goddamn!" Money XL roared as he emptied his scrotum inside Karel's welcoming orifice, shuddering like he had a seizure as he did so.

Karel hoped she got pregnant. It would be great to have a baby for him. They would forever be connected no matter what. Usually he would pull out and ejaculate all over her face or breasts, but tonight she got to enjoy the sensation of his juices caressing her insides. Money XL sat up in the bed catching his breath as both women snuggled up on either side of him.

"You had a great time?" Money XL asked Mindy, with a smile. He knew she had the time of her life.

"Oh my god...it was just incredible...I mean...I've fantasized about you for so long...and to actually..." Mindy grinned sheepishly and stopped in mid-sentence when she realized she was just rambling on.

Money XL's next question floored her.

"Do you have a visa? Are you able to travel to the States?"

"Yeah...I have a 10 year visa...doesn't expire for another seven years...why?" Mindy's mind was reeling. Could he really want to see her again? This was almost too much for her.

"I'd like for you to come and hang out with us from time to time. Matter of fact, my record label is throwing me a birthday party in Las Vegas next week...would you like to come?"

Mindy couldn't believe her ears. Her head was spinning.

"Most definitely," Mindy replied softly. She was in awe. It was like a dream. If it was, she hoped she would never wake up.

"Ok, cool. I'll send you a first class ticket to come to New York next Friday and then we fly down to Vegas on the company jet on Saturday. We'll exchange numbers before I check out. I'm leaving today at 2 p.m."

Karel looked at the time. It was now 7:30 in the morning.

"Time to get some shut eye hun," Karel told him.

"Yeah," he agreed and slid down on the bed to make himself more comfortable. It took Mindy about an hour to fall asleep. She wondered about Money XL's and Karel's relationship and how open they were sexually. She briefly thought about Ethan but was feeling too euphoric to dwell on him. She would deal with that later.

Karel was the first one up and she called room service to find out what was available for breakfast and went to take a shower. She woke up Money XL and Mindy when the food arrived. The trio dug into the Spanish omelets, saltfish fritters, Johnny cakes and fried plantains with gusto. They were ravenous. By twelve thirty, everyone had showered and dressed, and when they got downstairs, the rest of the entourage was there waiting.

"Talk to you later," Money XL said, as he gave Mindy a kiss in front of everyone. Karel then hugged her and then the entire crew hopped into the waiting vehicles and made their way to the airport. Mindy tried hard to suppress a smile as she walked over to the designated area where the taxis were parked. She hopped in the back of one and gave the elderly driver directions to her home. Mindy got home in fifteen minutes and immediately placed her cell phone on the charger, deciding not to turn it on until later in the evening. She then went into the bathroom to take a shower as she hadn't bothered to take one at the hotel seeing as she didn't have a change of clothing. Karel had offered to give her something to put on, but Mindy was too voluptuous to fit into any of Karel's size zero designer garb.

Mindy sang loudly as she showered, still on a high from the night's events. It was just unbelievable how fantastic things had turned out. She couldn't wait to tell Sharlene everything. Well, almost everything. Sharlene didn't need to know that she had fucked Money XL's security guard. As for Big Mike, now that she was close to Money XL, she would try to get his ass fired. *Sharlene is going to shit herself with envy when she hears that I'll be going away to spend time with Money XL*, Mindy mused with a smile as she gently washed her bruised vagina. Mindy dozed off after her shower and didn't awaken until seven o' clock. She turned on her cell phone and saw the ton of missed calls and text messages from the previous night. She noticed that Ethan's last attempt to call her was from 3:30 in the morning. He hadn't attempted to call her all day. That meant he must be really pissed. She decided to wait a little while before contacting him. Give him some time to cool off. She called Sharlene and they chatted excitedly for an hour before Mindy, showing off, told her she would catch up with her later as she needed to call Money XL to see if he got home ok.

Mindy got her pocketbook and retrieved the slip of paper that he had written his cell number on. She dialed the number and the phone rang to voicemail:

You have reached Thompson's Funeral Home, our office hours are 8:30 a.m. to 5:30 p.m. Your business is important...

Trembling with anger, shock, embarrassment and disappointment, Mindy flung the phone into the wall, shattering it to pieces.

The Hurricane

The powerful hurricane howled angrily as it moved slowly through the dark, deserted streets of Kingston at 18 mph, with winds packing a gust of 145 mph. The company that supplied the electricity to most of the island had shut down its power grids at 2 p.m. citing safety concerns. It was now 4:30 p.m. and Hurricane Dean had been unleashing his wrath on Jamaica for the past hour. The category four hurricane, the most dangerous to hit the island since 1988, had approached from the east, leaving a trail of utter devastation as it made its way west. St. Thomas, where it made its entry, was in very bad shape. Many people, who sensibly had evacuated their homes and were at designated shelters, would not have a home to return to. Countless houses had lost their roofs – some dwellings had even collapsed – and there were widespread landslides. Entire communities were also marooned, as the Yallahs River had overflowed its banks. Hurricane Dean had already claimed two lives and more would die before he finally departed.

Candice was blissfully oblivious to the destruction taking place outside of the small, two bedroom inner-city dwelling where she was currently on her hands and knees, with her ample ass shaking mightily, imploring Gary to fuck her harder. He was complying, gripping her wide hips tightly as he drove his thick tool in and out of her saturated plumpness with wild abandon.

Candice's husband was away at the Cayman Islands on business, and had been unable to get back to Jamaica before the hurricane's arrival. She had spurned her husband's suggestion that she stayed with his brother and his family for the duration of the hurricane. She had told him that she would be fine, but would welcome his brother stopping by to make sure everything was in order. Her husband had reluctantly agreed and Gerald, his brother, went by the house, checked the roof and placed ply boards securely over all the windows. He declared that he was confident everything would be fine during the hurricane and left. As soon as he departed, Candice packed an overnight bag and called a cab to take her down to Seaview where Gary lived with his younger sister and her two kids.

Gary was the captain and best all-rounder on the Seaview Cricket Team which was sponsored by the company of which her husband was the Marketing Manager. She had met Gary at the awards ceremony after the season had ended three weeks ago, where Gary had copped two individual awards. She had been instantly attracted to him and Gary, having noticed the many discreet glances she had been throwing his way all night, had discreetly slipped her his number when he conveniently passed her in the hallway leading to the restrooms. Later that night, after trying unsuccessfully to have sex with her husband – he had fallen asleep snoring loudly while she nibbled on his chest – she had called Gary. He had been hanging out on the corner with his friends from the community when she called. The conversation had quickly turned sexual, and Candice had manipulated her needy pussy with two pudgy fingers as she lay beside her snoring husband while Gary told her all the things he wanted to do to her voluptuous body from the minute he had laid eyes on her. Unfortunately, she wasn't able to give Gary a chance to back up his assertion that he would 'fuck her like she had never been fucked before' until a week after their initial conversation. Her husband had to stay overnight in Montego Bay for a conference and their son, Kyle, was spending three weeks with his aunt and her children in Tampa Bay, Florida, and she had taken advantage of the free time and met Gary at a small hotel on Sandringham Avenue where he had indeed lived up to his word. He was rough, demanding and virile, and she loved it. She had not gotten another chance to be with him until today. She felt bad for feeling this way, but thank God for Hurricane Dean. She would be locked down with Gary and his pleasurable tool for at least two full days. Priceless.

"Jesus...oh Gary...oh Gary...I'm coming..." Candice moaned loudly with her eyes tightly shut as she climaxed. Gary stopped thrusting when her orgasm rocked her voluptuous frame. He liked to feel the spasms as her pussy shuddered with pleasure. They switched positions and Gary entered her missionary style with her knees tucked and bent back against her shoulders. He maintained eye contact and his shadow was a blur in the soft glow of the three lit candles as he buried himself inside her deeply and forcefully.

"Oh yes! Just like that! I feel it in my throat!" Candice shouted as she scratched Gary's back painfully. He didn't mind. He liked it as rough as he gave. She could draw blood for all he cared.

***

Bruce, Candice's husband, checked the time as he sat in his hotel room in Grand Cayman watching updates on the weather channel. It was 5:45 p.m. Cayman was an hour ahead of Jamaica so it was 4:45 there. He picked up his quad band Blackberry Curve and called his wife. The call went through and the house phone rang without an answer. He then dialed her cell. It also rang out to voicemail. Bruce figured she was sleeping. Candice always wanted to sleep or have sex in rainy weather. He hoped she was ok, the weather channel was reporting that Dean was currently wrecking havoc in Kingston. He regretted not having demanded that she stayed with his brother's family. She should not be alone at a time like this. Bruce sighed and un-wrapped the ham, egg and cheese sandwich he had purchased at the hotel bistro before retiring to his room. Candice could be so headstrong sometimes. That element of her personality served her well in her job as assistant manager at a food processing plant, but it sometimes caused quarrels in their marriage when she refused to listen to him. The tall, wiry presenter was now saying that the next update would be in an hour. Bruce took a huge bite out of the sandwich and switched to a movie. He would try calling Candice again in another hour or two.

<hr/>

"Oh yeah...suck de cocky baby...bloodclaat..." Gary groaned as he enjoyed the feel of Candice's juicy lips and thick, knowledgeable tongue wrapped around his dick. She sucked him enthusiastically, moaning loudly as she did so. Gary gripped her braids tightly as he felt his climax approaching. Gary ejaculated with a primal roar as the large Julie mango tree at the side of the house careened dangerously from the force of the powerful wind before it gave way and crashed into the roof of Gary's next door neighbour, causing extensive damage.

"Mmmm....mmmm...mmmm" Candice moaned as she swallowed his juices, still sucking insistently even after he had expended his last drop.

"Alright babes, it done now..." Gary said, prompting her to erupt with laughter.

"I could've sworn I heard something outside," Candice said as she got up and went to use the bathroom. Gary watched her lustfully in the soft light. He just loved her large, voluptuous body. She was a big woman, but she wore her weight well. Ultra thick creamy thighs, a large rear end that jiggled invitingly when she moved, and a delightful pair of breasts that were a joy to hold, kiss and caress. He enjoyed being with her and she knew how to treat a man, but he was smart enough to know that no matter how caught up she got, it was highly unlikely that she would leave her husband to be with him. Anything was possible though, she really liked him and she struck him as a strong woman who would do what she wanted to if it came down to it. Only time would tell.

Candice thought about the situation as she urinated with a loud hiss. Her husband always told her she peed like a man. She liked Gary a lot and would love to be able to see him more often. He was fun to be around and the sex was off the chain. He made her feel young, sexy and desirable. The only downside was that he was a little rough around the edges and other than playing on the cricket team, was not employed; nothing that couldn't be fixed though. Candice sighed as she wiped. Her husband loved her and she supposed she still loved him, but the marriage had settled into a routine that had become tedious, predictable and boring. Work. Kid. Sporadic sex. Occasional outing. There was no passion and spontaneity anymore. Well, she would continue seeing Gary and watch how things unfolded. What was to be would be. They were snacking on potato chips and soda, and listening to the small battery operated radio when Gary's cell phone rang.

He looked at the caller ID and answered the call. It was his next door neighbour. The island's two cellular phone networks were holding up admirably during the hurricane.

"What a gwaan Junior?" Gary said.

"Jesus Christ Gary!" Junior exclaimed breathlessly. "Mi house ah flood out rude bwoy! De rassclaat mango tree inna yuh backyard nuh fall dung pon mi roof and mash it up."

Gary sat up in surprise. "Bloodclaat! Fi real?"

So that was the sound that Candice had mentioned hearing.

"Yeah man!" Junior said. "Mi an' Charmaine ah try fi salvage a few things an' mek a dash fi it over yuh yard. Yuh can put we up till de storm ease up?"

"Yeah man," Gary replied without hesitation. They could stay in the living room until the hurricane passed. "Yuh coming right now?"

"Right now!" Junior confirmed. He hung up and he and his live-in-love, Charmaine, grabbed the two bags they had hastily thrown their most important stuff in, and hurried over to Gary's house as quickly as they dared in the dangerous conditions. Luckily for them, they didn't have far to go. Gary watched for them through a barely cracked louver window and opened the door as soon as they reached his doorstep. They rushed in and Gary quickly forced the door shut which was no easy feat due to the ferocious wind.

"T'anks Gary," Junior said as he waved hi to Candice, wondering where he had seen her before.

"No problem man, yuh can go inna de bathroom an' change outta yuh wet clothes," Gary told him.

Junior and Charmaine then went into the bathroom to change, while Candice lit the two-burner gas stove to warm up the dinner that Gary had cooked earlier. That was one of the things she also loved about him. He was an excellent cook. He had prepared what he called 'hurricane food': boiled bananas, large cornmeal dumplings, Irish potatoes and spicy calalloo with codfish. Gary's sister and her two kids came out to the living room and everyone ate and listened to the latest updates on the radio. There was a lot of flooding taking place in Clarendon and the police had shot and killed two men who were attempting to loot a mini-mart in Vineyard Town in Kingston.

The kids were then sent back to bed and the adults sat around and played card games and dominos for a couple of hours. Gary's sister then went into her room and Gary and Candice retired to theirs.

"Yuh feel say dem will hear if we gwaan wid a likkle t'ing?" Junior whispered as his hand snaked down between Charmaine's robust legs.

"We...can't...do...that...suppose somebody come into the living room for something...it wouldn't look right..." Charmaine breathed, her actions belying her words as she spread her legs to give him more access.

Junior sucked his teeth and got on top of her.

"Yuh love fret too much...mi need fi release some stress...yuh nuh see de whole a de house mash up," Junior said as he pulled the zipper on his pants and inserted his dick inside her.

"Ohhh...alright...mmmm....but hurry up...mmmm," Charmaine whispered as she wrapped her strong legs around his back and pulled him deeply inside her. They were lying on the worn out rug next to the small coffee table. The last time she had had sex with Gary, it was in this same exact spot. She had climaxed twice. The memory turned her on immensely and she gyrated under Junior and flicked her tongue in his ear.

"Lawd... baby...mmmm...woi..." Junior groaned as he lost himself in the familiar but always pleasurable confines of Charmaine's fleshy orifice. They had been together for four years and Junior had never once cheated on her. His friends always teased him that he was a 'one burner' and that he was 'pussy-whipped' but he didn't care. Charmaine owned his heart and his loins. A few months ago, a friendly soccer game between the men in the community had erupted into a fight over what was perceived by Junior to be a dirty tackle on him by a guy known only as Toothless. Junior had jumped to his feet in anger and had treated Toothless to a vicious beatdown. Toothless, his pride wounded, had fired back verbally telling Junior that 'ah nuh mi yuh fi beat up...go beat up de man weh ah fuck yuh woman behind yuh back'. Junior, with blood in his eyes, had to be restrained by four men, while toothless, his bloody mouth in a wide toothless grin, scampered to safety. Junior never mentioned the incident to Charmaine, but naturally, she had heard about it. She wasn't worried though; there was no way Junior would ever take someone's word over hers. She had been only mildly curious as to who Toothless was referring - whether it was Gary or Steve, who owned a bar and restaurant in the community.

"It seems as if your sister doesn't like Charmaine," Candice remarked to Gary as they cuddled in bed. She had just called her husband and told him that everything was fine, that she was just sleeping the time away. After a little while, she had told him her minutes were almost finished and that the land line seemed to be down. He told her he would call her back on her cell immediately but she turned off her phone and went back to join Gary in the bedroom. She had gone into the bathroom to make the call.

"Hmmm...maybe ah jus' a woman t'ing," Gary responded nonchalantly, though he knew why his sister didn't like Charmaine. She had seen Charmaine leaving his bedroom one day and had been frosty towards her ever since.

Candice started stroking him languidly. His dick responded immediately like an obedient soldier.

"Ready for round two?" she asked huskily.

"Mi always ready fi you babes," Gary crooned as he caressed her breasts.

Candice giggled as she lowered her head and took him in her mouth. She was falling for the ghetto youth big time. They made love that night until they were both spent and sore.

❦

Bruce tried calling Candice back four times before he gave up. *Guess her battery died*, he mused. He called his brother, Gerald, whom he got with no problem, and asked him to check on Candice for him as soon as the roads were passable.

❦

The following day, the rain had eased up and they all ventured out to see how much damage Hurricane Dean had inflicted on the community. A lot of trees and power lines were down and there was debris strewn all over the place. Junior was not alone, two more houses close by had lost their roofs as well, and the

'Welcome to Seaview' sign at the entrance of the community, was now wrapped around a light pole. All in all, things could have been much worse given the size and strength of the hurricane. The latest newscast had said that Hurricane Dean was on his way to the Yucatan Peninsula and would not hit the Cayman Islands. Candice said a silent prayer thanking God for that. Her husband was there and the Cayman Islands always fared badly when hit by a hurricane. That meant he would be home soon, though not for another day or two as there was bound to be a lot of scheduling and rescheduling by the airlines as they attempted to sort out all the flights that had to be cancelled because of the hurricane. Originally, Candice had planned to spend two days with Gary but she felt she should go home today if possible. She would wait until the afternoon, by then she would know if the roads leading to her home were passable.

Charmaine and Junior went home to assess the damage to their property, while Candice and Gary milled about chatting with the throng of people who were out on the street for a few more minutes before going back inside to prepare some break-fast. Gary quickly whipped up a meal of fried plantains with sausages and bread, and made a pot of chocolate tea much to the delight of his two nieces.

"Why yuh going home today?" Gary asked as he nibbled on Candice's neck. After breakfast they had retreated to the bed-room and were now naked in bed. They were both insatiable. "Yuh sure yuh nuh want to stay another night?"

"I...do..." Candice breathed, "but... I need...mmmm... to go home...ohhh... and make sure everything is ok..."

Gary then claimed her lips in a searing kiss as they rolled all over the bed in a passionate frenzy. He then slid inside her with-out a condom and Candice looked at him but did not object. She never thought that his dick could possibly feel any sweeter than it already did, but feeling him inside her unsheathed was pure bliss.

"Ohhh... Gary...just... don't come inside...me...ok...baby... ohhh...god...fuck me...fuck me baby..." Candice moaned as Gary lay on his side and held one of her legs straight up in the air. "Mmmm...just like that baby...ohhh...god...damn..."

"Yuh love how de buddy feel baby?" Gary asked as he thrust powerfully inside her depths.

"Oh god Gary...it feels so good...so rass good...you know how to fuck me baby..." Candice said through clenched teeth. This position allowed Gary to go very deep. His dick felt like it was hitting her tonsils. Just the way she liked it. She wondered what she was going to do as she felt an orgasm rushing to the fore. She was becoming addicted to Gary.

Later on that day, at two in the afternoon, after a big lunch of boiled bananas, dumplings and mackerel from the tin, Candice reluctantly decided to go home. The route to her home was clear. On the midday news, the reporter had named the areas in Kingston that were impassable and Hope Road, where she lived, was not among the ones named. Gary borrowed one of his friend's CBR F4 motorcycle, and Candice, though scared, allowed him to use it to take her home. Gary was a skilled rider and Candice nervously enjoyed her first time on a motorcycle. She could see why some people were addicted to bikes; it really gave one an adrenaline rush.

She had left her overnight bag at Gary's, and did not let him take her directly inside the complex. It might raise some eyebrows if her neighbours saw her come home on a motorbike with a strange man. So she got off just down the street and walked the rest of the way. The electronic gate to the complex was open and she did not know the security guard that was the manning the security post at the gate.

"Hi, I live at apartment 2..." Candice said as she entered the complex, her voice trailing off in shock as the damage to the complex caused by the hurricane greeted her.

"Good afternoon," the guard replied. "It's really fortunate that you were not home Miss...you could have been hurt."

Candice did not respond as she walked to her apartment in a daze. The roof was completely gone. As was her neighbour's and another apartment a few blocks down. Her front door was wide open; the lock on the grill which had been pried open lay uselessly on the patio.

"There was some looting...thieves managed to get away with quite a lot before the police was notified. Andrew, the regular security guard, was found tied up in the booth. The police are questioning him at the station...just to make sure he wasn't in cahoots with the looters," the guard continued.

She hadn't even noticed that he had been walking with her. Candice was numb with shock. It had just never occurred to her that her complex would have sustained much if any damage from the hurricane. The complex was fairly new, having been built just a little over five years ago. What was not destroyed by the hurricane had been scurried off by the looters. It was a complete loss. Her legs felt three times their normal weight as she trudged slowly around the apartment, looking at the extent of the devastation. How the fuck was she going to explain this to her husband when she had told him that everything was fine? How would she explain not being here when all of this happened? She had never felt so lost and distraught in all her thirty nine years.

"Rassclaat!" she heard a familiar voice behind her exclaim. It was Gerald, her brother-in-law.

"Lawd Jesus...where are we going to stay until we get the roof fixed and the house cleaned up?" Charmaine asked Junior, as they took the wet mattress outside and placed it on two drums so that it could get some sun.

"Mi nuh sure yet...but we mus' can stay with mi bredda or Auntie Blossom 'til de house sort out," Junior replied. He would prefer to stay with his aunt as she had more space than his brother and she lived closer to his job. He worked in the binding room at a printery in Cross Roads. He would call them both in a little while.

"Candice! Yuh alright? Why yuh didn't call me and let me know?" Gerald asked. After checking the news and hearing that the route to Hope Road was clear, he had driven over to check on Candice. His brother was worried sick as he had only spoken to her once during the hurricane.

Gerald looked closely at Candice when he realized that she was acting strangely. He didn't understand her demeanour. She looked as if she was in shock. Why would she be in shock now? The roof obviously had blown off from yesterday. Something wasn't right.

"She just come back and find out man," the security guard supplied helpfully.

Candice shot him a hateful look.

"Just come back? From where?" Gerald asked incredulously.

Candice was looking at him with her mouth slightly agape, as she tried to figure out what to say. Gerald's cell phone rang and he answered it on the first ring.

"Hello."

It was his brother.

"Yeah, I'm over at your house now or what is left of it," Gerald was saying.

Bruce, who was getting dressed to go down to the hotel lobby, paused from tying his shoe lace. "What's left of it? What yuh mean Gerald?"

"Hold on, mek yuh wife explain. She's right here."

Candice was unable to take the phone from Gerald's out-stretched hand. It was as if she was paralyzed.

The Good Friend

anya was thoughtful as she languished in the rush hour traffic on Marcus Garvey Drive. It seemed as if the entire work force that lived outside of Kingston endeavoured to get home at the same time between the hours of 5 to 6:30 p.m. She had tried to leave a little earlier to get a head start on the traffic, but her garrulous supervisor had called an unnecessary meeting at four, which had, much to her annoyance, lasted until exactly five. She was an account executive at Caribbean Enterprises Group, a multi-faceted company that offered a wide variety of goods and services. Her mind was on Jason, a guy she had met a few blocks from her office in New Kingston during her lunch break, while on her way back to work. She was still trying to figure out why she had stopped when he beckoned to her. It was so unlike her to entertain advances from strange men on the street. He was cute though, and was well dressed in a very nice charcoal grey suit that fitted his lanky frame to perfection. She had informed him that she was in a hurry and quickly wrote down the straight line to her office, as well as her mobile number.

Her phone rang cutting into her thoughts. She reached over and turned up the air conditioning as she answered the phone. The evening heat was sweltering.

"Hello."

"Hi, trying to reach Tanya," the person said in a questioning tone.

"This is she," Tanya replied, wondering irritably why the stupid bus driver behind her insisted on blowing his horn loudly every few seconds. *Asshole. Did he think that the traffic would miraculously disappear or start flowing just because he blew his horn?*

"Hi cutie, this is Jason," he replied, adding in case she was in doubt, "we met this afternoon in New Kingston."

"What's up, Jason?"

"Nothing much, taking a smoke break so I decided to give you a call," Jason replied, taking a drag on his cancer stick as he leaned against the almond tree in the commercial complex where he worked.

"Ok, I'm in traffic heading home," Tanya informed him. "I take it you're still at work?"

"Yeah, no rest for the wicked as they say," Jason said, admiring a new Honda Accord that had just pulled up to pick up the sexy receptionist that worked at the auto supplies store on Block B. "You looked really nice, no way was I about to allow you to pass me. Those eyes..."

"Let me tell you something about me," Tanya said, grateful as the traffic crawled a few more meters. "I'm not really impressed by lines, it's kind of a turn off so please don't go there."

"Fair enough," Jason replied coolly, "but it's not a line and I'm not trying to run game...just simply telling you what attracted me to you. Your eyes look incredible."

Tanya conceded mentally that her light brown contacts looked really nice – gave her large eyes an even more exotic look.

"Ok, thanks," she said, accepting the compliment.

"So when can I take you out to dinner?" Jason asked, stubbing out his cigarette butt with his black, wing-tip Kenneth Cole shoes.

"Tell you what, Jason," Tanya said, as her cell phone started beeping. The battery was dying. She had forgotten, as usual, to charge it over the weekend. "Let's just confine our interaction to the phone for the time being."

This would be a new concept for Jason as his idea of taking things slow was sex by the second date. But he was flexible.

"Okay, that's cool," he responded. "No problem."

"Good."

"I'm gonna get back to some work so I'll call you later," Jason said, as he headed back inside the office.

"Alright, later then," Tanya replied as she terminated the call.

Jason thought about Tanya as he sat at his desk. The office was quiet now. Only he and Rita, one of the sales representatives, were still there. The office closed at five but he normally worked an extra two or three hours in the evenings during the busy period. It was winding down to the Christmas holidays and there were a lot of orders coming in for stuff like book covers, promotional fliers, posters, calendars, bookmarkers and business cards. Grafix Unlimited was a relatively small but highly profitable graphics business owned by Jason's eldest uncle. They were known for their quick turnaround and high quality work, and had a large corporate clientele. Jason worked there as the chief graphic designer and supervised the other three designers that were employed to the company. Jason also did his thing on the side, developing web sites for small businesses. He had his own website, www.jamwebdesign.com, where he promoted his work.

He liked the way Tanya looked: cute; caramel complexion; petite; low, curly reddish tint hair. He loved her eyes too, very alluring.

"Bye, Jason," Rita said as she paused by the door. "Sure you're ok by yourself?"

Jason looked up at her. He knew Rita wanted him. She had been dropping subtle and lately, not so subtle hints – like the other day when she stooped down directly in his line of vision to pick up a pen exposing her underwear – ever since she started working there two weeks ago. She was attractive and very curvy, and holding a very fleshy package between her legs if the glimpse he got the other day was anything to go by; but his uncle had made him swear not to have any more inter-office relations after he had caused four female employees – two receptionists and two designers – to resign over a two year period. They always got their heart broken and ended up leaving. Rita was tempting though.

She was young and saucy, and was like a ripe, rosy East Indian mango, begging to be picked.

"I'll be fine," Jason replied with a grin. "See you tomorrow."

Rita smiled seductively and let herself out. *It seems I'm going to have to rape his fine ass,* she mused as she opened the door to her six year old Nissan Sentra. It used to be her mom's car before she upgraded to a new Nissan Altima a few months ago. Her mom swore by the Nissan brand. Affordable and easy to maintain, she would always say. Rita decided she would seduce Jason before next week was out. She knew he was interested and was told by Ms. Brown, the lady who cleaned the office and prepared the coffee for all and sundry, about all the drama that had taken place between Jason and some of the women who used to work there. "Stay away from 'im chile" she had implored one day when they were alone in the kitchenette, "'im very nice but 'im love too much ooman." Her warning just made Rita want him even more. Maybe she could tame the wild beast.

Jason and Tanya spoke on the phone several times a day that following week. They were getting to know each other and Tanya began to look forward to his constant text messages and emails throughout the course of the day, plus the phone calls in the evening, which usually came when she was stuck in traffic. She found him funny and charming, and warmed to him very quickly. She couldn't recall having laughed more in recent years than she had over the past few days. On Friday, she called him on his mobile in the afternoon.

"Hi Jason." She was in the ladies room at her office checking her make-up before heading out to get some late lunch. Work had been rather hectic and she hadn't been able to take lunch until two hours past her usual lunch time.

"Hey you," Jason said, answering the phone on the fifth ring. "What's up?"

"I'm here, about to go grab some lunch. Are you in office or on the road?"

"I'm at office," Jason told her as he checked his email. He opened a message from one of his ex-girlfriends that lived in Atlanta. She was now in the army after migrating to the United States six years ago. She kept in touch with him regularly though she had moved on and was now engaged to the head chef at a trendy Atlanta eatery.

"Ok. When am I going to see you?" Tanya asked, "I'm going to forget what you look like if I don't see you soon."

Jason laughed in surprise. "Is that right...you were the one who wanted to take things slow so I was just waiting patiently until you felt comfortable."

Tanya laughed sheepishly. "I'm ready...to see you again that is..."

"Ok. How about we go out for drinks and a bite to eat tomorrow night?"

"That sounds good...what time?" She was surprised at how eager she was to see him. Tomorrow suddenly seemed like light years away.

"Say about 9...?"

"Ok, sounds like a plan. I'll talk to you later," Tanya told him as she exited the bathroom. *What should she wear?* She hadn't felt this excited in years. Felt like a school girl and not a sophisticated thirty-one year old divorced mother of two young adorable boys who were the apple of her eye. Their father resided in Miami, and they had been divorced for the past three years after seven years of marriage. The last relationship she had been in was with an older guy. He was the only man she had ever been with apart from her husband.

She had a strict childhood growing up and her high school boyfriend had never gotten past first base. Not that she hadn't wanted to, but her mom's dramatic declarations of "If yuh ever come in this house wid nuh belly mi ah go kill yuh" and "Study yuh book an' nuh pay boys nuh mind, dem only want one t'ing" would deter her even when she was throbbing with lust and desire. The relationship with Cedric, who was ten years her senior, had been good for the most part. They went out regularly, he treated her well, and while the earth didn't move when they made love, it had been okay sex. She had cared about him deeply and had been shattered when she discovered that he was sleeping with several other women while he was with her. She had inadvertently found out about one and he had broken down and confessed to two others when she confronted him. They had spent so much time together she wondered where he had found the time to entertain all these women. But she supposed where there's a will, there's a way. He was still trying to get her back. She had sworn off men in the nine months since the break up, but Jason had awakened that fire in her again. He gave her a reason to smile these days. Hopefully he would also give her a reason to wear all that sexy lingerie she had in her drawer at home. She hadn't gotten laid in so long she was beginning to feel like a born-again virgin.

She couldn't believe she was thinking like that so soon. Normally sex was put on the back burner until she really got to know the person. It had taken Cedric three months of dating to get into her ultra tight honey-pot. He had been beside himself the first time they made love. It was like he had died and gone to pussy heaven: "Oh fuck...yuh tight eeh" and "Jesus...lawd... baby...how inside ah yuh sweet so?" She knew her pussy was prime meat. Her husband used to behave the same way and had literally lost his mind when she had cut off the sex in the latter part of the marriage. He went ballistic. He had smashed the windows in her car – twice; kicked down doors; created numerous scenes in public...you name it. He still, after three years apart, had not gotten over the divorce. Sometimes she thought she hated him, but mostly she felt sorry for him. Crazy bastard.

Jason left work at 7 that Friday evening and went home to relax. He wasn't sure what his plans were for the night, but he knew he would be going back on the road. He lived alone in a two bedroom apartment on Wilmington Crescent. When he got home, he stripped down to his boxers and made himself a drink. Armed with his mix of Hennessey and Red Bull, and a pack of cigarettes, he reclined on his easy chair in the living room and switched on the television. He turned to Fox Sports World to catch up on all the sports highlights. His cell phone rang when he got up to replenish his drink. He looked at the caller ID. It was Andrea. He had met her a few weeks back in the parking lot of one of Kingston's most popular nightclubs. They had spoken on the phone several times since then, but he hadn't gotten a chance to see her again. She was a business major in her second year at the University of Commerce and Technology.

"Hi sexy," Jason said as he filled his glass with ice.

"Hi Jason, what's up?" Andrea was in the drive through at a fast food joint getting some chicken. Her best friend, Carol, had her dad's car for the weekend as he was away in Trinidad on business. She had wanted to see Jason for some time now, but she had been busy with school projects and she was very focused on her work. She had to maintain a high GPA as she hoped to get a scholarship to do her Master's after completing her first degree. With her projects completed and all assignments handed in on time, she was now ready to have some fun. She hoped Jason was free tonight.

"I'm good...at home chilling...watching TV and having a drink." He lit another cigarette and wandered out to the verandah. The sky was grey. Not one star in sight. A heavy downpour was definitely on its way.

"What are you doing tonight?" Andrea asked, signaling to Carol who was placing the order at the intercom that she wanted the number 2 combo.

"Not sure yet," Jason told her.

"Want some company?" Andrea purred. Her boyfriend, a final year medical student at another University, was at a pool tournament with his friends despite the fact that they hadn't been able to spend much time together over the past week due to their hectic schedules. *Well, lucky him*, Andrea surmised. She wanted some dick tonight and she hoped Jason's cute ass would oblige.

Jason thought for a moment. He had kind of lost interest in Andrea as he didn't like when too much time elapsed before he got to see a girl again after the initial meeting, but tonight was as good a time as any to get reacquainted. It was about to rain, he didn't have any concrete plans, and from what he remembered, she had a long pair of sexy legs that he wouldn't mind tying in a bow around his neck.

"Sure," Jason responded, "where are you now?"

"I'm on the road with my friend getting some food. I'll just let her drop me off by you and you take me home later."

"Ok, I live at 21 Wilmington Crescent," Jason told her. "The main gate will be open so just tell your friend to drive in. I'm at apartment four."

"Ok, cool. See you in about fifteen minutes," Andrea said and hung up the phone. She slipped off her sandals and placed her lanky legs on the dashboard.

Carol looked at her. "What the hell are you so pleased about?"

Andrea laughed. "Remember that cute guy I met a few weeks when we went clubbing?"

Carol frowned. "In the parking lot?"

"Yeah..."

"Oh, yeah...the one you acted like you wanted to go home with..."

Andrea giggled and slapped her friend's arm playfully.

"No, I wasn't acting like that!"

"Yes you were...I had to blow the fucking horn like four times before you decided to come on," Carol retorted as she drove up to the pick-up window.

"Whatever...your ass was cockblocking," Andrea teased.

"Girl please...I wanted to sleep...hold this and shut the fuck up," she said, dumping the bag of food in Andrea's lap.

Andrea grinned and sat up a bit so she could rest the bag properly in her lap. Carol was right though, she wanted to fuck Jason the moment she met him. The real reason she hadn't left with him was because she had spotted her boyfriend's cousin in the parking lot. She had been standing about six cars away with two of her friends, eating jerk chicken, and watching her. They hadn't acknowledged each other as Andrea didn't like her; too nosy and snobbish. She took a sip of her soda as Carol headed down Hope Road. It had started drizzling.

Tanya was home relaxing. The kids were on the carpet watching cartoons and she was lying down in the couch doing a crossword puzzle. She wondered what Jason was doing. She checked the time and picked up the phone. Rochelle, her good friend who lived in New York, should be home from work by now.

Rochelle picked up on the third ring.

"Hey girl!" she said excitedly when she realized it was Tanya. Tanya had been her best friend for several years now. "What's up?"

"Heeyyyy," Tanya replied jovially, "I've got news!"

"Spill it girl!" Rochelle was pleased to hear Tanya sounding like that. She had gotten way too serious over the past several months. It could only mean one thing.

"Well, I met this guy..."

"I knew it was a man!" Rochelle broke in triumphantly. "I just knew it! Your ass sounded too happy for it to be anything else and I know you hadn't won the lottery."

Tanya laughed heartily. "Whatever! Anyway, as I was saying, I met this really cute guy the other day and we've been talking on the phone and stuff...he's really nice Rochelle...intelligent, charming...and did I say cute?"

"Yes, you did," Rochelle replied laughing. "Sounds good. How old is he?"

"Twenty-seven..."

"What! You've never been interested in younger guys before...this guy must be something else," Rochelle remarked.

"I know...I know... but trust me, he's very mature for his age. I'm going out with him tomorrow night. Nothing big...just going to have some food and a few drinks."

"Okay...I'm happy to hear that you've met somebody that you really like. Have you told him about the kids and your crazy ass ex-husband?"

"Well, I haven't really gone in depth about Donovan, but he knows about the kids."

They chatted for an hour on the phone and then Tanya put the kids to bed and went into her bedroom to masturbate. Telling Rochelle all about Jason had gotten her juices flowing. She retrieved her trusty red vibrator from the bottom of her lingerie drawer, and settled in for what she just knew was going to be an amazing orgasm.

Jason's cell phone rang on his way back downstairs. After talking to Andrea, he had gone upstairs to take a shower.

It was Andrea. Jason, shirtless in a pair of boxers, socks and slippers, stepped out on the patio. The rain was now falling quite heavily. Lightning flashed twice, briefly illuminating the dark sky.

"I'm outside," Andrea said needlessly when Jason answered the phone.

He could see the car idling behind his Subaru Imprezza. Jason told her he didn't have an umbrella so she would have to make a dash for it. He also told her it was ok if her friend wanted to come in and chill until the rain eased up. When rain fell this heavily in Kingston, water quickly accumulated on the road in some areas due to the inadequate draining system.

Andrea told him ok and ended the call.

"Jason says you should probably come in and chill until the rain eases up," she told Carol.

Carol didn't really want to be a third wheel but the prospect of driving in the heavy rain all the way up to Manor Park where she lived was a daunting one.

"Ok," she agreed, and they gathered their things and ran as fast as they dared to the verandah. Carol squealed, much to Jason's amusement, when a violent streak of lightning struck as they reached the verandah. He ushered them inside the apartment and closed the front door. Despite the short distance from the car to the verandah, the girls were soaked.

"Rass man," Carol bemoaned, "My hair is messed up." She had gone to the hairdresser earlier that day to get her hair done for the weekend. Carol was high maintenance. Her hair and nails had to be done weekly without fail and a new outfit had to be added to her wardrobe at least every two weeks. Fortunately, her father was relatively well-off and doted on his only daughter. She had recently written off the car he had bought her eight months ago and he had told her she would not be getting another before she graduated. With two years to go, Carol found that unacceptable. She knew he would soon get tired of her pestering him to use his car and cave in and get her one. She wanted one of the new Suzuki Swifts. She thought they were so cute.

Jason told them to make themselves comfortable. Andrea sat beside him while Carol sat across from them on the other sofa. The girls dug into the food they had purchased while Jerome sipped his drink and lit another cigarette. He turned up the volume as the sound of the rain was making it difficult for them to hear the television, and switched the channel from sports to music.

While eating, Carol looked across at Jason to tell him he had a nice apartment and happened to see the mushroom head of his dick peeking out the leg of his boxers against his thigh. She choked on her chicken sandwich. Jason jumped up and went over to her, slapping her hard on the back a few times until the food dislodged itself from her throat.

"Yuh alright, girl?" Andrea asked through a mouthful of hot wings.

Carol nodded and asked Jason for the bathroom. He told her it was the middle door upstairs and she scampered up the stairs quickly.

"Your friend seems a bit uncomfortable," Jason remarked as he sat back down next to Andrea.

"No man...she's alright," Andrea answered, though she did think that Carol was acting a bit jumpy.

Carol went inside the bathroom and locked the door. The bathroom was small, but was very clean and smelled fresh. She couldn't believe she had choked on her food like that. It was so embarrassing. At least they didn't know what had caused her to choke. She moved her hand down to her crotch, touching her pussy to make sure it was still there. She swore it had jumped out of her panties when she had glimpsed the bulbous head of Jason's cock. Her legs felt weak. She sat down on the closed toilet and after a moment's hesitation, slid her panties to her ankles. Carol closed her eyes and started to masturbate.

Andrea finished eating and Jason took the empty food containers into the kitchen and placed them into the trash can. Andrea lit up a cigarette and asked Jason to bring her a drink. He brought her a bottle of Smirnoff Ice and she placed her feet on the coffee table and took a long swig. She felt very relaxed. And horny. Jason was sitting very close to her and had started to gently nuzzle her neck. She was extremely sensitive there. She moaned softly.

"Your legs are so sexy," he murmured, in between licks to her ear. "Can't wait to find out how being between them feels..."

She placed her cigarette in the ashtray and reached down to run her hand along the length of his dick through his boxers.

"Mmmm..." Andrea moaned appreciatively. Jason's cock was the prefect blend of length and girth. Her pussy felt hot. She parted her legs slightly and took another swig of the cold drink.

She wondered absently what the hell Carol was doing in the bathroom so long.

"I wonder if Carol is ok," she murmured, as she nibbled along Jason's prominent jaw-line.

"I almost forgot she was here," Jason replied, "I'm going to see if she's ok."

"Looking like that?" Andrea said laughing and pointing at his crotch. Jason's boxers resembled a large tent.

Jason grinned. "Matter of fact...let's both go upstairs..."

When they got upstairs, they paused by the bathroom door. It sounded like Carol was crying softly.

"Carol?" Jason called out. "You ok?"

Carol was in the throes of her second orgasm when she faintly heard Jason's voice. It intensified her climax and she shook violently on the toilet seat, fervently trying to keep quiet.

After he called her a third time, this time knocking on the door, she answered in a shaky voice that she was ok. That the chicken had upset her stomach but she'd be fine.

"Ok, we'll be in my room for a little while if you need us," Jason told her, and pulled Andrea inside his bedroom. He closed the door behind him as Andrea jumped on to the bed. He joined her and gave her a searing kiss. She moaned in his mouth and wrapped her legs around him, holding him in a tight embrace. They kissed until they were both gasping for air. Jason rose and quickly removed her skirt. Jason uttered a guttural grunt when he saw the front of her white panties. It was soaking wet. Andrea gasped when he literally ripped them from her body and threw it in the air behind him. It caught on the ceiling fan and stayed there. She eased up and quickly removed her top before he tore it off as well. It was a Seven for All Mankind peasant blouse and one of her favourites. Jason hurriedly discarded his boxers and freed his raging erection. He knelt between Andrea's legs and placed one on his right shoulder while he held the other straight in the air, kissing along its length.

Andrea groaned with anticipation as he slowly worked his way down to her throbbing pussy. Her body was on fire and crying for release. He put her legs down and settled comfortably between them. He licked the insides of her thighs languidly, and Andrea moaned loudly as he blew softly on her clit and licked around the fringes of her lower lips. She tried to pull his head down directly on her pulsating wetness but he restrained her hands and continued to tease her.

"Oh god Jason," she moaned. "Eat me please...please make me come...oh god...I'm going crazy..."

Jason ignored her pleas for another minute before he softly flicked his tongue back and forth over her protruding clit. He then started licking her clit so fast Andrea swore she got a lick for every raindrop that fell outside.

"Yes! Fuck yes!" Andrea shouted as she squirmed beneath his knowledgeable tongue.

Jason spelled her name on her clitoris twice before sliding his tongue inside her slippery wetness as far as it would go. Andrea howled with pleasure as she flooded Jason's mouth and face with her secretions.

<hr />

Carol had exited the bathroom and was on her way downstairs when she heard Andrea moaning loudly. She had stopped and listened by the door and was so turned on she almost went in. She sighed and made her way downstairs. The rain had eased up somewhat and she decided to let herself out instead of disturbing their fun. It would have been nice if she could've joined in and sampled Jason, but she wasn't into women and wouldn't want to have to touch Andrea. What good was a threesome if all the participants didn't interact with each other? She found the padlock on the kitchen table and pulled up the door and locked the grill. It was drizzling slightly as she made her way to the car. She whipped out her phone and searched for Leroy's number. He was a street guy that she had met at a party on campus a few months ago and they had hooked up a few times. She felt for his brand of sex of sex right about now. Rough and hard. She wanted to be pounded into oblivion. She was so horny her pussy ached.

❧

"Fuck me Jason!" Andrea implored through clenched teeth. Jason was plunging inside her from behind while she balanced herself by holding on to the chest of drawers.

"Mmmm...fuck this pussy!" she commanded, reaching around to slap his ass and urge him on. "Ohhhh...mmmm...oh yeah..."

Jason had been pleasantly surprised at how vocal and fun she was in bed. He definitely planned to keep seeing her every now and then. She was a true tigress. He gripped a fistful of her almost shoulder-length hair and quickened his pace as he felt his scrotum tightening. Andrea felt his eruption approaching and coaxed him the rest of the way.

"Come for me Jason...oh yeah...wet my pussy up...fill me up Jason...fill me the fuck up...oh god..."

Jason's roar was primal as he ejaculated, thrashing wildly inside her as he filled the latex condom with his seed. When he went to the bathroom to dispose of the condom and returned to the bedroom, Andrea was still in the same position holding on to the chest of drawers with her ass poking out. It had been that good.

❧

The following morning, after giving the kids breakfast and dropping them off at their Grandmother's, Tanya went to the hairdresser to get her hair and nails done. It was packed, as usual, and Tanya settled in for what she knew would be at least a half-day affair.

❧

Jason got up around 11 a.m. and Andrea, who had ended up spending the night, made them a quick breakfast of scrambled eggs, toast, and spicy jerk sausages straight from the can. Andrea, originally from St. Elizabeth, lived on one of the four female dormitories on campus. Jason dropped her there at a few minutes after 1 in the afternoon and then went to the barber to get a hair-cut. Andrea turned on her cell phone as she made her way to her room on the second floor and checked her voicemail. Her boyfriend had left four messages, and her mom, one. She sat at her desk and switched on her computer as she returned their calls.

That night, Jason arrived at Tanya's home in Portmore at 9:15 p.m. He called to let her know he was outside and she came out three minutes later. Tanya walked to his car, feeling excited. She was wearing a baby blue halter top with a pair of snug black pants and black slippers. She had changed three times before deciding on what to wear.

"Hi, Jason," she said, as she climbed into his car and shut the door.

"Sup babes," Jason replied, eyeing her appreciatively. "You look great."

"Thanks," Tanya responded, giving him a quick hug. *Damn he smelled good.* "Looking good yourself." And he was. Jason had on a very nice white Armani Exchange casual dress shirt with the sleeves rolled up at the elbows, and designer jeans. The vibe was mellow and tinged with anticipation as they headed to Kingston.

Jason took her to 3D, the latest hangout spot on the hip strip in New Kingston. The food was excellent and while it was usually packed, it was spacious and service was quick. They settled in one of the few vacant booths and a waiter was there almost immediately to take their order. Jason ordered Jerk Pasta – a spicy pasta dish served with grilled jerk chicken, bell peppers, mushrooms and onions in a callaloo cream sauce, while Tanya decided on Chicken Quesadilla filled with pepper jack cheese and served with salsa and sour cream.

Tanya was enjoying the evening immensely. The food was absolutely delicious and Jason was really good company. They talked about any and everything, and she was surprised to know that Jason was an avid chess player. She had always associated that game with nerds. An hour and a half later, after dinner and drinks, which Tanya had been careful to limit to two glasses of white wine, they made their way out to the parking lot. Tanya felt slightly nervous as they went into the vehicle. Her mind and her body were waging a brutal war. She wanted Jason inside her in the worst way but her mind was adamant that it was too soon. Much too soon. Like a boxing fan watching a bout at ringside, she wondered who would win.

"Had a good time?" Jason asked, as they sat in the vehicle. He didn't turn the engine on and left his door ajar.

"I had a great time," Tanya replied; sitting with her legs tightly crossed.

"Are you ready to go home?" Jason queried softly. They both knew what he was asking. He ran his fingers lightly along her right arm.

Tanya uncrossed and crossed her legs again. She tended to do that when she was nervous.

"I think I should," she replied, turning her big eyes on Jason. They were brimming with desire.

Jason abruptly got up and went around to the passenger side. Without even thinking about it, she opened her legs and he sat between them. With total disregard for the people walking about in the relatively brightly-lit parking lot, Jason kissed her. It was a gentle kiss that lit a thousand fires in Tanya's body. If she didn't go home right this minute she was going to fuck his brains out.

"I need to go Jason," Tanya sighed reluctantly, when he finally broke the kiss.

Jason knew that if he pushed it she would come home with him but he decided to chill. He really liked her and didn't want her to have any regrets.

"Ok," he replied, and kissed her on the forehead. "I'll take you home."

The ride back to Portmore was mostly silent, though not uncomfortably so. They both knew it would be on and popping the next time they saw each other.

Tanya called Rochelle on Sunday and filled her in on the date with Jason. Rochelle told Tanya she did the right thing by controlling herself on the first date, and that she thought it was a good sign that Jason hadn't pressured her. They chatted for awhile, and Rochelle informed Tanya that she was considering taking a two week vacation soon. Rochelle was planning to start an online retail business and if it panned out, she planned to return to Jamaica permanently. She hated living in New York and she hated her job. She was the personal assistant to the managing director of an upscale clothing store and the woman was a demanding, unreasonable pain in the ass. Tanya suggested that she should take a look at Jason's website as that was part of what he did for a living. Maybe he could be the one to set up her online venture. Rochelle wrote down the name of Jason's website and told Tanya she would have a look at what Jason had to offer. They chatted awhile longer and then Tanya hung up and went into the kitchen to prepare dinner. It was Sunday and the kids would riot if they didn't get their rice and peas and baked chicken followed by ice cream. She checked the time. It was 12:50 p.m. She should be finished cooking by 3.

Rochelle went jogging in Riverside Park – she found it more relaxing to run there than Central Park – and when she returned home she took a shower and then went online. Her overweight feline, Oprah, rubbed against her bare feet purring softly, vying with the computer for her attention. She rubbed Oprah with her toes absently and logged on to Jason's website after clearing her email. She was impressed. The site was very professionally done. It looked great, was very easy to navigate and pretty much answered any question she could think of asking. He would be perfect to design her site. She clicked on the 'Contact Us' tab, and sent him an introductory email. She concisely told him what she had in mind, and asked him what would be his turnaround time and estimated cost for him to develop her site. She didn't mention that she knew Tanya. Business was business; down the line if he indeed was the one she commissioned to do the job, then the fact that she and Tanya were good friends would come to light. She clicked on the 'About Us' tab and there was a picture of Jason along with a mission statement. It was a head shot of him seated around a desk in an office. *He really is very cute,* Rochelle mused. *Tanya has done well.* She looked at the picture awhile longer and hoped that he wouldn't break her friend's heart.

Tanya thought about Jason all day at work. She kept thinking about their kiss. It had felt so good. She wanted him. Badly. At 3 p.m. she called the helper to let her know that she would be home a little late this evening. She spoke to the kids for a few minutes and told them to ensure that they did their homework as she would be checking when she got home. She then called Jason. It occurred to her while dialing his number that perhaps this was the first call she should've made. Suppose he wasn't available to see her this evening?

She listened impatiently as his phone rang out to voicemail. She left a brief message asking him to call her as soon as possible.

Tanya then tried to do some work while she waited for him to return her call. She was annoyed at herself for not being able to concentrate. She had no idea why this intense desire to sleep with Jason came over her today. She just *had* to see him. Jason took her out of her misery ten minutes later.

Tanya answered on the first ring.

"Hey sexy, sorry I missed your call...I was in a meeting," Jason told her.

"That's ok," Tanya said. "I want to see you after work this evening...will that be possible?"

"Sure...we can link up any time after 6," Jason replied.

Tanya didn't even realize she had been holding her breath until she exhaled with a sigh of relief.

"Great," she replied, knowing she sounded a bit too excited but was too horny to be embarrassed. She didn't have to touch herself to know that she was dripping. She could feel the puddle in her panties. Good thing she had on stockings as well. "So I'll call you at 6 for directions to your house."

"Ok, babes. Later then." Jason smiled as he terminated the call. She sounded really enthused to see him later. Desperate almost. This evening should be very interesting. He checked the time. It was 3:08. He then logged into his email account for his website business and checked his messages. There were five messages: three from existing customers and two from prospective customers. He responded to all of them and then began working on a project he had to do for the Sports Institute of Jamaica. They would be hosting an important track and field meet in three months time and wanted a website developed to promote the event. Jason figured he would work on that for the next couple of hours before leaving to meet with Tanya.

Rochelle checked her email as she enjoyed a glass of white wine while Oprah contentedly slurped her milk from the fancy bowl that Rochelle had bought for her at a quirky store in the eastside of Manhattan. Dennis, a guy she had met on 74th Street a few days ago, was coming to pick her up at eight. They were going to see *Prelude to a Kiss*, one of the current plays on Broadway. She was going to give him the 'Oprah test'. If her cat didn't like him, then his ass was grass. The last two guys Oprah hadn't liked had turned out to be assholes. She never heard from one again after she gave up the goods and the other had been way too possessive. After those two experiences she decided she would trust Oprah's instincts. If Oprah displayed any hostility, she would go out with him and enjoy the play, but she would never see him again. Jason had responded to her email. *That was quick*, Rochelle mused. All the information she wanted was there. It would cost her three thousand US dollars for Jason to design and implement the site. Once the 50% deposit and all the relevant information was provided, he would have the site up and running in 14 days.

She wrote him back thanking him for his prompt response and that she would get back to him shortly. Rochelle then retrieved her dirty clothes basket and made her way downstairs to the laundry room that served the apartment building. Her date was a little over two hours away so she had time to do a load or two.

<hr/>

Tanya was filled with nervous excitement as she turned on to the street where Jason lived. She hummed along to the soulful track playing on the radio as she came to number 21 and pulled in behind Jason's car. He came out on the patio to greet her.

"Hi sexy," Jason said as he hugged her tightly when she reached him.

"Hey," Tanya murmured softly, loving the way she felt in his arms.

He then led her inside the apartment and closed the door behind them.

"Would you like anything to drink?" Jason asked, stopping at the foot of the stairs.

Tanya shook her head in response. Jason then lowered his head and kissed her gently.

"Mmmm..." Tanya moaned in his mouth as she deepened the kiss. Jason shrugged off her jacket and pulled the buttons on her blouse as he freed her small breasts.

"Oh Jason," Tanya murmured as he bent his head and started nibbling on her breasts. She had unusually large nipples and they were very sensitive. Jason latched on to the right one and sucked it like a new born baby as he pulled her belt and unbuttoned her pants. When he slid his hand in her panties, she was soaked.

"Ohhh...ohhhh...mmmm...yes...yes..." Tanya moaned loudly as his thumb found her clit. He then slipped his index finger inside her wetness. She arched her body against his and cried out as an unexpected orgasm rippled through her petite frame. Jason then placed her to sit on the stairs and she lifted her legs as he pulled off her pants and panties in one fluid motion.

"Sweet Jesus..." Tanya breathed as Jason knelt down and started licking her slender thighs, working his way down slowly and tantalizingly to her anxiously waiting pussy. She wasn't used to oral sex the first time she made love with a new partner but hey, she wasn't going to stop him. She placed one of her legs on the wall and hooked the other in the staircase as she allowed him all the access he needed. Jason placed his hands under her ass and lifted her to his mouth. He moaned as he nibbled on her fleshy lips and inserted his tongue as far as it would go.

Tanya screamed with pleasure as he tongue-fucked her.

"Don't stop! Don't stop! Don't fucking stop!" Her toes literally curled as she climaxed for the second time that evening. "Oh my God!"

Jason then rose and quickly stripped off his shorts. His dick was turgid and slick with pre-cum. Tanya decided he deserved a treat and she sat up and pulled him towards her by his dick. She rubbed her thumb over the slit, liking the slippery feel of his semen. She opened wide and took his entire swollen, pulsing dick in her mouth. Jason assumed a wide legged stance and looked skyward as she deep-throated him.

"Fuck...damn baby...pussyclaat...Tanya..." Jason groaned with pleasure as Tanya took his scrotum in her mouth while she pumped his shaft with her tiny hands. "Mmmm...that feels so good girl..."

"Fuck me Jason," Tanya said, looking up at him with her big innocent eyes as she released his dick and stood up. She turned around and bent a little, holding on to the wall and staircase for balance.

Jason groaned and quickly went downstairs for a condom which he hurriedly placed on his dick as he made his way back to her. He positioned himself behind Tanya and inserted his dick slowly until he was buried to the hilt.

Tanya grimaced. She was sure if she looked down she could see it poking through her ribs. He had a nice sized dick and it felt even bigger than it looked. Filled her right up and then some. Jason slapped her ass as he ground his way in and out of her slowly and deeply.

"Mmmm...so tight...and sweet...oh fuck..."

Unable to restrain himself any longer, Jason upped the tempo and started to really pound Tanya. His balls slapped noisily against her thighs as he gripped her tiny waist and drilled her pussy mercilessly.

"Fucking hell! Jesus Christ! Jason! Are you trying to kill me? Oh God!" Tanya wailed as she tried to allow him his moment of wildness. She knew from past experience that men went berserk when inside her. Apparently her pussy had a special ingredient that made it sweeter and more succulent than the average woman's. It wouldn't be much longer before he climaxed. She had already gotten hers, twice, so she didn't want to mess up what she knew would be a very explosive orgasm for Jason.

She arched her back even more so he could go even deeper if it was humanly possible. Apparently it was. She emitted a piercing cry as Jason seemingly soared to new heights. He was impossibly deep, hitting corners and crevices that have never before seen the light of day much less a dick. Tanya started saying things she had never before uttered in her life.

"Violate me Jason! Tear my pussy up! Yes! Fuck it 'til I can't recognize it! Jesus Christ!"

Her words drove Jason over the edge. He was caught in that bitter sweet moment when a man is enjoying the sex so much he wants to climax but he doesn't want to climax. He feels it coming and welcomes it, but also wishes he could hold it back. Jason roared as he climaxed, his teeth clenched and sweat pouring off his athletic body as he filled the latex condom with his seed. He continued to clutch Tanya, and shivered for a long time after he ejaculated. Never in his young life had he experienced such an intense orgasm.

Rochelle's date arrived promptly at eight. She was applying the last of her make-up when the door bell rang. She gave herself a final once over in the full length mirror in the hallway and went to get the door. Oprah was already by the door, waiting expectantly. Rochelle shook her head and smiled. That damn cat was just too smart for its own good.

"Hi Dennis," Rochelle said, stepping aside and allowing him to come in.

"Hi Rochelle, you look amazing," Dennis gushed as he stepped inside and kissed her on the cheek.

"Is this your pretty cat?" he crooned, as he stooped to pet Oprah. She hissed and gave him a nasty scratch on his hand.

"Ouch!" Dennis said as he recoiled. "Guess she doesn't like me very much."

"Oprah!" Rochelle chided. "Behave! Let me see that... hmmm...nasty scratch. Let's get this cleaned."

Dennis sat on the sofa watching Oprah warily as Rochelle went and got some peroxide and a band-aid. She cleaned the cut and covered it with the band-aid.

"Ready to go?" she asked, smiling apologetically.

"Yeah, thanks," Dennis said.

Rochelle got her pocketbook and they exited the apartment. She signed inwardly as they took the elevator down to the ground floor. *Yet another one fails the Oprah test. Oh well, at least I'll enjoy the play,* she mused. *God I need me a man.*

The play was excellent and Dennis was ok, if boring company. He was trying too hard to be *nice*. It was damn near annoying. He seemed a bit peeved that she didn't invite him in for a night cap but left without protesting too much. Oprah was happy to see her when she returned. She changed quickly into boy shorts and a tank top and checked her messages. Tanya had called her twice, imploring her to call when she got home, even if it was two in the morning. Rochelle grinned. That could only mean one thing. She had given up the goods. She reclined on her tan leather loveseat with Oprah in her lap, and a glass of white wine, and called Tanya. This promised to be an entertaining conversation.

Tanya was in her bedroom listening to love songs with the lights off when Rochelle called. She had gotten home at 8:30 and had looked over the kids' homework before putting them to bed at 9. Mildred, the helper, had been grumpy as Tanya had told her she would have been home by 8. She had left for home as soon as Tanya walked through the door. Tanya answered on the first ring.

"Hello."

"Hey T, what's up girl?" Rochelle said, sipping her wine.

"Girl, I've been trying to reach you...you went out?" Tanya asked, sitting up and switching on the bedside lamp.

"Yeah, remember I told you I was going to the play with Dennis? He failed the Oprah test by the way."

Tanya laughed heartily. "Another reject. Well, at least *I've* got good news...I had sex with Jason today and girl...it was fucking incredible."

Rochelle laughed in surprise. Tanya rarely cursed. For her to use an expletive to emphasize how good it was, Jason must have really blown her back out.

"Wow...guess he really laid the pipe down the real and proper way," Rochelle said saucily.

"I'm a bit sore but trust me...I'm not complaining," Tanya said contentedly.

Rochelle laughed. "Come on girl...give me more details! How many times did you come? How big is his dick? Where did you guys have sex?"

"My god...you want a blow by blow commentary?" Tanya asked jokingly.

"Shit yes! I'm not getting any right now...I'm living my sex life vicariously through you...how crazy is that?" Rochelle teased.

Tanya laughed in agreement. Usually Rochelle was the one with the colourful sex life. They chatted for over an hour before they got off the phone. Tanya went straight to sleep while Rochelle switched on her laptop and went online. She went to Jason's website and looked at his picture again. He really was fine. Tanya had told her she was falling for him big time but had some reservations. She was a little wary of Jason. So smooth and handsome. Was he a player? Rochelle decided to give Jason a test.

✦✦✦✦✦✦✦✦

Jason got to the office at ten the next morning. He was feeling pleased with himself. He had secured a lucrative freelance designing contract with a new mobile company. He would be responsible for designing their website among other things. He had met with them at 8:30 and the meeting had gone exceptionally well. His uncle didn't mind that Jason pursued his own business on the side. He knew that Jason would not short change him and was good at managing his time. Besides, Jason was also his favourite nephew and he wanted the very best for him. He was handed eight messages by the receptionist and he spent a few minutes returning calls as he cleared his email. There was a message from the woman who was interested in getting him to design her website. It read:

Hi Jason,

Hope all is well. Thank you for your prompt response in sending me the quotation. I'm currently reviewing it and will get back to you. By the way, I had a look at your photo on the website. You are quite handsome. Your girlfriend must feel very lucky. Have a great day.

Rochelle

He responded:

Hi Rochelle,

Thanks, for the compliment. I don't really have a girlfriend per say at the moment. Looking forward to hearing from you once you have reviewed the quotation. You have a good day as well.

Jason

After corresponding by email throughout the day, Jason called Tanya as he usually did while she was languishing in traffic to go home. She was thrilled that he was maintaining his usual behaviour after they had had sex. Some men tended to change immediately after getting the prize, especially so quickly. They chatted for a bit and made plans to see each other the following day. Jason worked late that evening and Rita, the sexy new sales rep, stayed behind as well to work on some reports or so she said to Melanie, who was hoping to catch a ride home with her as they lived in the same direction. Jason, caught up in what he was doing, didn't even know that she was there. At six-thirty, he got up from his back cubicle to get a red bull from the kitchenette.

"Hey you...I didn't know I wasn't alone," Jason remarked, stopping by her desk. It was the first time he was seeing her all day. She had been on the road when he came in that morning.

"Hey handsome....just finishing up some reports...I'll be leaving in a little while," Rita replied, treating Jason to a hundred watt smile.

He returned her smile as he looked at her ripe, voluptuous body spilling out of a smart navy blue skirt suit. The skirt was rather short and she was wearing stockings and trendy Aldo pumps. Jason had overheard some of the other girls gossiping about Rita, and apparently it was assumed that Rita was a spoiled brat who didn't have any responsibilities and spent all her money on clothes and partying. *Well*, Jason surmised, *it was money well spent*. Rita always looked hot and sexy.

"You look nice..." Jason remarked, his eyes lingering at her chest. She had unbuttoned two of the buttons on her inner blouse, displaying some cleavage.

"Thanks...I didn't think you even noticed me..." Rita said, pouting sexily.

"I try not to..."Jason replied.

Rita decided that this was the moment she had been waiting for. She got up from her desk and strutted to the front door. Jason watched in resignation as she locked the door and pulled the shutters. He knew he should stop her, nothing good ever came of these office affairs, but his dick had other ideas. He was already erect. Rita, still standing by the door, slipped off her jacket and placed it on the receptionist's desk. She then slipped off her pumps and pulled off her stockings. She eased her blouse out of her skirt and pulled all the buttons. She hiked her skirt around her waist and assumed a wide-legged stance as she licked her juicy, lip-gloss laden lips at Jason. She wasn't wearing any panties. Jason's dick lurched at the sight of her young, plump, shaven vagina. It was a beautiful sight. Jason groaned and pulled out his dick.

"Oh my God..." Rita breathed, "Just as I imagined it...what do you want me to do with that big dick Jason... huh...you want me to suck it...you want me to ride it...anything you want Jason..."

Rita was pushing all the right buttons. Jason rushed over to her and she jumped in his arms. He held her against the door and she wrapped her legs around him. They kissed passionately as his cock probed the entrance of her wet pussy. Caught up in the moment, there was no thought of any condom. He entered her with a firm thrust and she gasped in his mouth.

"Oh Jason...your dick feels so good...I've wanted you for so long...give it to me Jason...fuck me..." Rita moaned. She couldn't believe it was finally happening. She had wanted Jason from her first day at work. That it was happening at the office further added to her excitement. The office door rattled from their exertions. Rita started to squeal as she climaxed and drenched Jason's cock and the front of his slacks with her juices.

"Yesssss...yessssss...yessss..." Rita moaned in a hoarse whisper as she quivered in his arms. "Mmmmm....oh fuck...so good...mmmm...."

She didn't come a moment too soon as Jason increased his tempo and shot a torrid load of semen inside her willing orifice.

"Oh Jason...wet up my pussy baby...mmmm...your cum feels good baby...mmmm..." Rita groaned as Jason grunted and shuddered in ecstasy. He withdrew from her slowly and she stood up unsteadily.

"I really enjoyed that," Rita said, as she sat on the edge of the receptionist's desk and caught her breath.

"Yeah...I shouldn't have ejaculated inside of you though," Jason said. "We can't be playing around like that...next time we'll use protection."

"Yeah..." Rita agreed, though secretly she wouldn't mind getting pregnant for him. The baby would be cute as hell and Jason had money, so it would be all good. "Don't worry though...I'll get a morning after pill on my way home."

"Ok, cool." Jason then went into the kitchenette to get a can of red bull. He didn't feel like working anymore so they locked up and left together.

Rita was all smiles as she made her way up Oxford Road. She couldn't wait until they had sex again. She hadn't even gotten a chance to show him her oral skills. She could suck a mean dick. She would blow his mind. She laughed at the pun as she turned up the radio. Fifty Cent's bumping new single had just come on.

Jason was thoughtful as he headed home. He would keep seeing Rita but he would have to tell her to keep things on the hush. His uncle would be furious if he found out. Rita was a very good sales rep; she had drummed up quite a bit of business for the company in the short space of time she had been there. He would not want to lose her and besides, Jason had promised him to leave the staff alone.

***

Hmmm, Rochelle mused as she checked her email. *So he doesn't consider Tanya to be his girlfriend...interesting.* It was not looking good already. She decided to push a little harder and see if he would bite. She didn't want her best friend to become a statistic. She had been through enough lying and cheating with her last boyfriend. Rochelle responded to Jason's email and told him that she probably would wait until she came to Jamaica in another month or so before she gave him the deposit to start developing the website, but she was definitely going to use him. She also told him that seeing that he didn't have a girlfriend, it would be great if he could take her out when she came to Jamaica. She told him that it was probably unfair that she knew what he looked like and he had no clue as to her appearance, but that he should fret not, he could bet six months salary that he would like what he sees. She hoped he answered tonight. She fed Oprah and then went to take a shower. She took one of her vibrators with her. She was horny.

***

"Hi J..." Tanya drawled. The kids were in the living room watching cartoons and she was sitting on the patio looking out at the neighbourhood guys playing soccer on the open lot across the street.

"Hi baby," Jason replied brightly. "What's good?" He was in the kitchen making a ham and cheese sandwich when she called.

"Nothing much...you ran across my mind so I decided to give you a call," Tanya said. Actually, she wanted to talk to him about something.

"Ok, I'm here making a sandwich," Jason replied.

"J...listen...I'm a big girl right and I don't have time for games...I *really* like you and I need us to put some definition to what is going on."

"Ok..." Jason saw where she was going. She wanted a serious relationship.

"I'm not seeking a father for my kids or anything like that, but if I'm sleeping with someone it has to be in the context of a relationship. If we are going to continue seeing each other, I have to know that I'm your woman. Your *only* woman."

Jason took a swig from the bottle of Gatorade that he was having with his sandwich and sat on the kitchen stool. He wanted to continue seeing her so there was no choice but to agree.

Tanya held her breath as she waited for him to respond. It scared her how much she wanted him.

"Ok," Jason replied, after a moment of thought. "I want you in my life so that's it. Let's give it a shot."

"Ok, great," Tanya said, trying valiantly to keep the note of relief out of her voice.

"I'm gonna take a shower now babes, so I'll catch up with you later," Jason told her.

"Alright baby, later then."

"Yes!" Tanya shouted when she came off the phone.

Evan and Errol, her two sons, rushed out to the patio to see what their mother was shouting about.

"Yuh alright mummy?" Evan, the eldest queried.

"Yes sweetheart," Tanya replied, smiling as she pinched his cheeks playfully. "Mommy is just happy."

<hr/>

After taking a shower, Jason went online to check his email. He read the email from Rochelle and smiled. He told her that it was great that she would be coming to Jamaica soon and that he would be happy to show her a good time during her visit. He then got dressed and went on the road to check some of his friends. They usually hung out at a sports bar on Hagley Park road.

<hr/>

After two weeks of flirting with Jason, by which time the emails had gotten quite steamy, Rochelle decided she had found out all she needed to know. Jason went to work one Monday morning and checked his email. There was a message from Rochelle. He froze when he read it.

Let me introduce myself, I am really the best friend of the girl you are seeing and I know it was a wrong thing to have done but I needed to know if you had her best interest at heart. When you get this mail, she will already know as I called her early this morning. I had to tell her.

Why are you doing this to my girl? Though she was a bit concerned that you might be a player, she is so in love with you and is excited at the prospect of a future with you. I had told her after what happened in her last relationship she probably should give men a long break and she was in the midst of doing just that but then she met you and fell hard. She is my girl so I decided to see if you were a good man.

It turns out that I am the one she's upset with, not you. She really loves you and I hope you both can sort things out, she's not answering my calls so I don't know. I am sorry but I think I am saving her from herself.

Jason read the message three times. He then went into damage control mode. He quickly responded to her email.

Lol...I knew it! Trust me, I just wanted to see how far you would take it before the truth came out. I knew it was either that or a prank. You probably think you have done her a good deed but its sad, because shes not going to believe me after this. You have caused her a lot of pain for no reason. I know you meant well but this just shows that it's never wise to meddle.

Then he wrote Tanya:

Morning baby,

I knew it was a prank the moment she started getting personal. I thought that it was my ex trying to pull a stunt or someone that I knew or that you knew. Either way, I was just going with the flow until the truth came out cause it obviously had to. You may not believe me but I definitely knew it was a hoax. Think about it babes. Why would I put myself out there like that for someone on the internet? I mean, it could be anybody. Your friend probably meant well but all she has done is cause you pain. I don't regret having played along as it was all a big joke to me. My only regret is that right now you are hurting because you think I'm a dog and I don't care about you but that's not the case baby. Think about it carefully before you decide not to have anything to do with me. I'll wait to hear from you. I love you baby.

Tanya called him half an hour later.

"Why has my best friend and my man put me in this position?" she said when Jason answered the phone. "Who do I believe? How do I know you weren't up for it but is now trying to lie your way out because you got busted? How do I know that she doesn't really want you but got cold feet?"

Jason was silent.

"This is so crazy," Tanya continued. "I'll call you back later after I've thought things out. My head is spinning. Bye."

Jason shrugged his shoulders and put the phone down. He didn't want it to be over between them but if she didn't see it his way then there was nothing he could do. He settled down and got to work. What a way to start the day. He wasn't used to all this drama.

<hr>

Rochelle was distraught and unable to concentrate at work that day. She faked illness to go home early. Her boss was unsympathetic but told her to go home as she was about as useful as an asshole on her elbow. She couldn't believe that Tanya would not take her calls or respond to her emails. She had cursed Rochelle out when Rochelle told her what she had done and basically accused her of wanting her man. Life was so crazy. Well, she was going to Jamaica next week; hopefully Tanya would talk to her then.

<hr>

"Oh God baby! Yes! Oh fuck! I'm coming!" Tanya announced as she bounced up and down Jason's dick like a trampoline.

"Who fucking you? Huh?" Jason growled as he slapped her ass.

"You baby! My big dick man! Ohhh!" Tanya replied, squeezing her breasts as she climaxed.

There was no sex like make-up sex. After thinking about the

situation for a long time, Tanya decided that she would believe her man. Rochelle had probably gotten the idea in her head to sample Jason after she saw how fine he was and heard how good he was in bed. Traitorous slut. She would never speak to her again. She had then called Jason and told him she would meet him by his house after work.

Jason then flipped her over and entered her doggystyle. Tanya crawled further up the bed with each powerful thrust and Jason, not relenting, crawled right with her until she was trapped in the corner by the wall.

"Fucking hell baby! You trying to break it off inside me? Jesus Christ!" Tanya groaned as Jason fucked her like it was the last time he would be having sex.

"Whose pussy? Eh?" Jason asked as he squatted over her and dug in even deeper.

"Yours baby...mmmm...all yours...fuck out it rass!"

Jason uttered a guttural roar as he pulled out and ripped off the condom. He turned Tanya's head and sprayed his thick juice all over her face.

Tanya moaned with her eyes tightly shut, marveling at how hot it felt against her skin.

"You look like a porn star," Jason remarked with a grin.

Tanya laughed and they went to take a shower together. All was well again.

* * *

Ten days later, Jason, after working late to finish up a project, locked the office up at 8:30 and went out into the parking lot. There was a tinted, white Toyota Camry next to his car. He glanced at it curiously before opening his car and putting his laptop and pouch on the backseat. The driver door to the car next to him opened and a short, attractive woman stepped out.

"Hi Jason," she said softly, as she walked around to stand in front of him.

She opened her coat. She was naked underneath. Her nipple rings and navel ring glistened in the moonlight. Jason watched dumbstruck as the woman touched herself and showed him her finger. It was slick with her juices.

"See how wet I am for you?" She licked the finger sensously.

"Was I right? Do you like what you see?" Rochelle asked as she grinned devilishly and squatted in front of Jason.

He braced against the car and looked up at the starry sky in wonder as the combination of her warm mouth and the cold metallic tongue ring sent ripples through his body.

He never saw when she took out the knife from her coat pocket.

Printed in the United States
123266LV00005B/3/P